THE ESCAPE ACROSS THE OCEAN

Riya
Musthyala

To all my friends, family, teachers and readers

This is the story of a 12 year old girl called Heather and a 10 year old boy called Nate

Contents

Chapter 1
Spring holidays

"I'm looking forward to spending the Spring Holidays in Northern Oak Town!"

"Me too! It will be so fun!"

Nate and Heather are brother and sister, Nate is ten years old and Heather is twelve. They both live in a wonderful town called Oak Town and love absolutely everything about it!

At the moment, it is the first day of their Spring holidays and they are getting ready to go to their grandparents' house for the break; their Grandparents live in the North.

The North of Oak Town is mostly dense woods and forests while the South is warm and busy and has one of the three police departments; in the West there are shops, parks, cinemas and Oak Town's largest school; the East is home to the Mayor.

Heather and Nate live in the Southeast. The Southeast is calm, yet lively and has many shops and fun things to do. Oak Town has many lakes, streams, fields, trees however, it is best known for all of its... Oak Trees! The townsfolk love the trees, it's almost as if the whole town is built around them! It's currently Spring and the North of Oak Town looks gorgeous in the weather. Heather and Nate are going to be going there...

"I wonder if we are going to have anymore adventures these holidays!" pondered Nate, carelessly stuffing his belongings into his suitcase.

"I doubt we will," sighed Heather.

"You're right, but an adventure sure would be fun!" Nate thought.

In their Autumn holidays last year, Heather and Nate went on an adventure... They were on a mission to save their beloved town from a gang of three thieves who were stopping at nothing to get what they wanted.

Heather and Nate found the place where the thieves were hiding the goods that they had stolen and when they went and told the police they didn't believe Heather and Nate, so they refused to help. It was unfortunate as all the police officers in Oak Town are very nice except for one (the one who was on duty at the time Heather and Nate went to the police department).

Fortunately, that police officer was fired and some new officers were recruited. But, after Heather and Nate were sent away from the police department, they decided they would go to the place where the thieves were hiding the stolen goods and film it so they could take it to the police department and show it to them as evidence. However, two of the thieves were in the hideout at the time so they saw Heather and Nate interfering... They then took them to their lair and held them captive until Heather and Nate handed over the camera footage that they had of the thieves' hiding place for stolen goods. Heather and Nate managed to escape and flew away in a hot air balloon. At the same time, they cleverly managed to trap the thieves! But soon after they flew the hot air balloon away from the thieves' hideout, Heather and Nate got lost…

Then, they soon saw a little cottage in the distance and went to ask the owner if they knew the way back to Oak Town. The owner of the cottage was a kind old woman called Mrs Bird and she helped them both get back to Oak Town using a map that she had made herself! When they got back to Oak Town, they went to the police department and with the help of the police they captured the three thieves… And…

They saved Oak Town!

On top of that, Heather and Nate were awarded a special award called Oak Town's Award of Gratitude! It is an award given to chosen people by the Mayor and is an honour to be given one. This was Heather and Nate's first adventure and they hoped for many in the future…

"We are going to have so much fun in the North!" smiled Heather.

"Definitely!" agreed Nate.

Heather and Nate's Parents have to attend an emergency business trip so Heather and Nate had to spend the holidays in Northern Oak Town, with their Grandparents...

"Hurry up, Nate! We are going to have to go soon!" Heather reminded.

"Oh yes, sorry!" Nate apologised.

Oak Town is a very environmentally friendly town as it is ninety percent car free! So, only a few people own cars, meaning the air is very clean. The town is also very safe for children as everyone knows one another.

Heather and Nate were going to be taking the train to their grandparents' house. After some deliberation, Nate managed to pack all his belongings into his suitcase, neatly!

"Come on then! Let's go!"

Chapter 2

Journey to Northern Oak Town

"So then, have you both packed everything you will need for Grandma and Grandpa's house?" Mum asked, looking at their suitcases.

"Yep."

"I think so."

They replied.

"Well, if you're all set then we might as well get going!" Dad announced.

"The train is scheduled to leave in twenty minutes from Southern Oak Town Station and it will travel straight to Northern Oak Town Station," informed Dad.

"Ok."

After that, Heather, Nate, Mum and Dad left the house and began walking to the train station. Emerald, green vegetation swayed in the cool spring breeze and fluffy white clouds lazily glided through the bright, sapphire sky...

Soon, they arrived at the station and went to the platform to wait for the train to arrive.

"How long until the train arrives?" pondered Nate.

"Just ten minutes or so," Mum replied.

"Ok."

"I wonder if we will have any adventures these holidays?" Nate thought out loud.

"Oh Nate! You have said that around ten times already!" sighed Heather.

"I know but won't another adventure be exciting!" exclaimed Nate, thinking back on all the fun they had in their previous adventure.

"I certainly hope you don't have another adventure!" interrupted Mum.

"I agree, you can't stop an adventure from coming but you can stop yourself searching for them," Dad said, informatively.

"That's true," Nate acknowledged.

"Yeah."

"Oh look!"

"That's our train!" spotted Dad.

"Come on everyone!" he exclaimed, leading the way into the carriage of the train.

The train was a shade of deep ruby red with streaks of gold and *'Oak Town Express'* emblazoned across the side.

The family found their seats and the train was off!

"I can't wait to see Grandma and Grandpa again!" exclaimed Heather.

"Me too," said Nate.

"We'll try and come back as soon as possible," Mum told them, upset that she would have to have the business trip right in the middle of the spring holidays.

"Look!"

"I think we're nearly there!"

"There's the station in the distance!" exclaimed Nate, eyeing the station that was quickly up coming.

"Oh yes!"

"There it is!" exclaimed Heather, getting excited as well.

"No matter how many times we come here I always get excited!" admitted Heather, ecstatic!

After a short while, the train pulled up in the station and all the passengers made their way onto the platform.

Heather and Nate looked around and grinned. Then, Nate spotted a porter on the other side of the platform. He had shaggy brown hair that fell on his mostly hidden face; he was dressed in the regular porters' uniform but from what you could see of his face it seemed oddly familiar.

"Heather, look," said Nate, pointing at the man.

"What?" Heather asked her brother.

"Does that man seem familiar to you?" Nate asked her, racking his brain as to why he recognized this person.

"He does seem oddly familiar," Heather replied, not thinking much of it.

Nate on the other hand was mightily confused and was pondering where he had seen this person.

"Is this going to be the start of another adventure?" he asked himself.

"Heather, Nate, hurry up!" called Dad.

"We need to make a move on!" Mum added.

"Coming!" they called back.

But little did they know that they would have another adventure…

Chapter 3

Arriving at Grandma and Grandpa's house

Heather, Nate and their family casually ambled to Heather and Nate's Grandparents' house.

"The North of Oak Town is very different to the Southeast," observed Nate, looking around.

"Yes, it is," acknowledged Mum.

"There aren't these many Oak Trees back down in the South," Dad added.

Then, they began walking to their Grandparents' house…

"Are we nearly there yet?" Nate grumbled, for the hundredth time!

"Nate, we have only been walking for five minutes!" laughed Heather.

"But it feels like five hours!" Nate groaned.

"Nate! We aren't even carrying anything!" Heather replied, noticing her brother's free hands.

"Oh yes, luckily!" Nate laughed.

At Oak Town train station, the staff had a special service where all you had to do was to write your address on a sticker that was put on your luggage; and it would be delivered to your house for you to save you the trouble of carrying your luggage. This was done as in Oak Town hardly any people own cars so a large majority of the population walked everywhere!

"We will be at Grandma and Grandpa's house soon!" Mum declared.

"Oh good!" announced Nate, his stomach rumbling.

After another couple of minutes of walking, the troop reached their destination! Grandma and Grandpa's house was a beautiful house and was near town. There were jolly postmen delivering letters and milkmen delivering milk! There were shops of all sorts and everyone was always smiling and greeting one another with a cheery wave. The house was on the edge of town, so, to the other side of it there was a large field and even further, a dense wood...

Heather and Nate ran to the house and knocked on the large oak door...

Chapter 4

Meet Grandma and Grandpa

The door was opened and the family was greeted merrily.

"Welcome!" smiled Grandma.

"We really have missed you all!" said Grandpa, lovingly.

"Come in!" invited Grandma.

Heather, Nate, Mum and Dad followed Grandma and Grandpa into their lovely little home and they all sat around the blazing, warm fire that was burning in the fireplace.

After a catch up, Mum and Dad had to go.

The family said their final goodbyes and then Mum and Dad left for the station.

DING DONG

Came the noise as someone rung the bell.

"Ah, that must be your luggage," Grandpa informed, getting up from his seat to get the door.

Heather and Nate followed and then collected their luggage but the porter who handed it to them was the same one that they recognized back at the station.

Nate took a small step back and Heather gulped.

The porter's eyes widened at the sight of Heather and Nate and for a split second scowled but then put on a neutral face for Grandpa.

"Here's your luggage," he wisped in a low voice as if he was trying to disguise it.

"Thank you very much," smiled Grandpa, looking over to Heather and Nate waiting patiently for them to say thank you!

"Heather, Nate, what do you say to this kind porter?" Grandpa gestured, slightly taken aback by their dignified silence.

"Thank you."

"Thanks."

They both said quietly.

The porter smiled a broad smile but Heather and Nate knew something was up... They recognized the porters face and it made them feel unsafe and unsure.

Soon, the porter left and Heather and Nate went back into the living room.

"Heather and Nate, you two must be very tired," Grandpa said to them.

"You've had a long day," he added.

"We're not that tired," Nate ushered, noticing the time was only seven fifteen!

"Yeah," Heather added.

They weren't tired, they were just puzzled and confused. Who this strange man and why did he seem dangerously familiar?

"Let me take you to your bedroom," offered Grandma, coming out of the kitchen.

"Yes please," Heather replied.

"Thank you," Nate added, warmly.

They followed Grandma up to their bedroom and went in happily.

The room was on the top floor of the house and was large yet cosy with a slanted roof and skylight windows. It was painted a shade of warm cream and had daylight streaming in. There were two single beds both with light knitted blankets and fluffy pillows. There was one large wardrobe and one smaller one. And, set of oak bookshelves that stretched round a corner and was packed with books.

"I love this room!" smiled Heather.

"Me too," Nate grinned

The room smelt of lavender and summer flowers.

"I'll leave you two to unpack a bit and then I'll come to collect you for dinner," Grandma smiled, warmly.

Then, she handed them their luggage and left the bedroom, happy that her grandchildren were around.

Heather and Nate began talking as soon as she was out of earshot.

"Nate, you're right, there was something about that man that made him seem familiar."

"Yeah," Nate replied.

"Did you see the way he looked at us for a split second?" Heather asked, hoping she wasn't the only person who saw the look.

"Yes, I did," Nate said.

"I thought I imagined it, but clearly not," pondered Nate.

"It was like he recognized us but we didn't recognize him," he added.

"Yes, that's true," Heather acknowledged.

Heather and Nate unpacked in silence as they knew they were both thinking about the same thing – who was this mysterious man…?

After a while, Grandma came upstairs and called them down for dinner. It was a delicious meal! There were jacket potatoes, baked beans, home-grown salad, loads of cheese and plenty of lemonade!

"This is the most delicious dinner ever!" complemented Heather, between sips of lemonade!

"It certainly is!" added Nate, loving every bit of it.

"We're glad you like it!"

"Thank you very much," replied the Grandparents.

They all ate happily and chatted even more happily!

After the meal, Heather and Nate and their Grandparents played a board game before going to their room, brushed their teeth, changed into their pyjamas and then went to bed. They fell asleep as soon as their heads hit the pillows…

Chapter 5

Going into town

The next day Heather and Nate woke up to the sound of birds chirping and the warmth of the sun streaming onto their beds from the large open windows...

"Good morning, Heather," yawned Nate.

"Good morning, Nate," Heather replied.

After a couple of minutes, Grandma came upstairs and told Heather and Nate the plan for the day.

"Good morning you two! Today, I'm planning on taking a walk into town to get some fruit and veg from the market and string and the weekly newspaper from the post office! You can come with me if you want!" breathed Grandma.

"Wow, of course we will come!" exclaimed Heather!

Nate nodded.

Grandma smiled at their enthusiasm.

"We can pop into town straight after breakfast if you would like..." planned Grandma.

"Yes please."

"That sounds great!"

"Thanks Grandma!"

"My pleasure, now, brush your teeth and have your baths while I make your breakfasts," instructed Grandma, cheerily.

"Okay."

"Thank you!"

Heather and Nate groggily got out of their beds and did their morning routine…

Soon, they went downstairs for breakfast, there were hot pieces of toast smothered in butter and jam, bagels, scrambled eggs and salt and pepper, waffles, strawberries and yogurt!

"Mmm," grinned Nate, looking at the plates of hot and cold food.

"Wow, this is amazing!" smiled Heather.

"Thank you," beamed Grandpa, happy that the breakfast went down well with the children.

"Now, let's not wait any longer! Tuck in!"

Heather and Nate helped themselves to portions of the delicious food and ate happily! They all had an amicable conversation and laughed merrily! After they finished eating, Grandma told Heather and Nate they would now be going into town. But, little did they know who they'd see once more…

Chapter 6

Shocking news

Heather, Nate and Grandma walked through town and stopped off at various places like: the fruit and veg market, the florists, the milkmen, the butchers and they were now on their way to the final shop which was the post office...

"What do we need from the post office, Grandma?" asked Nate, curiously.

"Hmm, let's think, we need a copy of the weekly newspaper, I need to post a letter and a parcel to your aunt, we need some string, some tape," announced Grandma.

"That sounds great!" Heather replied.

"Look, there's the post office!"

They walked into the post office and Grandma said she would wait in the line to drop off her parcel and letter, while Heather and Nate could collect the weekly newspaper from the rack at the back of the shop.

Heather and Nate went to the back of the small shop to collect the newspaper when they saw a familiar face once more.

The man they had kept seeing was in the storeroom at the back of the shop! This time he was wearing a shop keepers' uniform (a white shirt, a brown blazer and a red and brown striped tie) but what he was wearing was a shirt so dirty it no longer looked white, a brown blazer with lots of holes and a tie that was formerly white but had red and brown stripes painted on it; and he was writing something on a note whilst snarling menacingly.

"Nate, look," whispered Heather, sleekly, pointing at inside the storeroom.

Nate gasped, forgetting to be quiet!

The man sharply looked out of the storeroom, shoving the note in his pocket.

"Who's there?" he asked, hoping they hadn't seen what he was writing.

Nate nudged Heather.

"Oh, we don't mean to be any trouble, we were just looking at the array of newspapers here," gestured Heather.

The man confidently walked out of the storeroom and looked at them closely, his eyes widening.

"It can't be," he said to himself, quietly, he was clearly surprised.

"What can't be?" Heather asked him, wanting to get to the bottom of this.

"Oh, nothing," he said, trying to push past them.

But Heather and Nate stood there firmly.

"Tell us why you said 'it can't be', what do you know about us?" Nate asked.

"Oh, it was just that I remember you from last year, when you saved Oak Town," he said, but Heather and Nate knew there was something more than that as there was a flicker of danger in his eyes and he was trying to cover up why he recognized them.

He tried to push past again.

"Wait, why are you dressed as a shopkeeper?" Heather asked.

"I thought you were a porter at the station. We saw you yesterday there," she added.

"Oh, well that's because I'm trying new jobs in the area," he blurted.

Heather and Nate were going to continue interrogating the man but their Grandma was calling them and so they grabbed a newspaper and went back to her.

"Well done for getting the newspaper!" Grandma said to them, warmly.

"Now you two, let's get the rest of the items and then we can go home," announced Grandma.

Heather and Nate rushed around the small yet full shop and swiftly collected all the items on Grandma's list before putting them on the till to be paid for.

After that, they walked home…

When Heather and Nate went home, they did some gardening and then went upstairs to their bedroom.

"Heather is it just me who senses another adventure!" smiled Nate, mischievously.

"I think we will have another one too," Heather replied, pondering the recent events.

And, they were right, another adventure was coming along…

Chapter 7
The counterfeit money

After a while, Heather and Nate went downstairs for some lunch and the newspaper was sitting on the table. They sat down and Heather and Nate began to read it. Before he gasped. His mouth was open very wide and his eyes were filled with shock.

"Nate, what's wrong?" asked Heather.

"Look!" Nate pointed at the extract in the newspaper.

This is what it looked like:

COUNTERFEIT MONEY BEING CIRCULATED THROUGH OAK TOWN

MYSTERY CRIMINALS ON THE LOOSE

"Counterfeit money being circulated through Oak Town – mystery criminals on the loose," Heather read to herself out loud.

She looked at Nate.

"Nate, I think this might be an adventure," announced Heather, with mixed emotions.

Nate grinned.

"Let's hope this is one for us to have, not for someone else!"

Heather shook her head, smiling.

Heather and Nate had loads of fun that afternoon and before they knew it, it was getting dark.

"Heather and Nate can you two do a job for me?" asked Grandma.

"Yes, sure."

"Okay."

They replied.

"Thank you."

"So, can you both go up to the attic and fetch my old violin; my friend would like to borrow it," Grandma told them.

"Okay, we'll go and get it."

They both went up to the top floor and then went up into the attic.

"Wow, I never knew Grandma and Grandpa had such cool stuff!" exclaimed Nate, looking around.

"Look, that must be the violin," said Nate, pointing at a dusty red violin case that was propped up against a wall.

"Oh yes."

They went to get the violin when Nate spotted a cool leather case on the windowsill. He went towards it and opened it. Inside was a magnificent pair of binoculars.

"Wow! Heather look at these!" said Nate, waving the binoculars at her.

"Nate! Be careful! That dust is getting everywhere!" coughed Heather.

"Sorry."

Nate put the binoculars to his eyes and to his amazement they were astonishingly good!

"Wow Heather! You have to try these; I can see the tiniest specks of dust close up!" exclaimed Nate, excitedly.

Heather put the violin case down for a moment and took the binoculars from her brother.

"Woah, these are amazing!" Heather exclaimed, grinning in amazement.

"We will be able to see miles out into the distance with these!" she added, excitedly.

"Let's look out of this window," Nate decided, pointing at the small, round window at the far end of the room.

Nate went first and looked out the window...

"Wow Heather, I can see things that my eye alone can't dream of!" gasped Nate.

"Here, you try."

"You're right Nate, I can see far off into the distance," grinned Heather.

"Look, I can even see an abandoned house in the middle of the fields bordering Oak Town from Willow Town," gaped Heather.

"What?" asked Nate, thinking that he had heard wrong!

"Look, Nate, there's an abandoned house; well, it looks abandoned. It's in a terrible state," observed Heather.

"Can I see?"

Heather handed Nate the binoculars and told him where to look…

Then, Nate saw it.

"You're right, it is in a terrible state."

"It is half covered with vines and the other half is all ruins," Nate examined.

They took it in turns to look at the house; it was fascinating to see the little birds nesting in the vegetation and to see the rabbits bouncing around it playfully. Until, Heather spotted something that sent shivers down her spine…

"Heather, are you alright?" asked Nate, seeing that Heather was very startled by something that she saw.

"What did you see?"

"Nate, I, I saw," stuttered Heather.

"You two! Are you alright up there?" called Grandma.

"Yes."

"Yeah, we are just on our way down," Nate said on behalf of both of them.

"Tell me in a minute," he said to Heather.

Heather just nodded – she was speechless.

Heather and Nate left the attic and gave Grandma the violin; she thanked them heartily.

Then, they had some free time before dinner so they told Grandma that they would go to their bedroom to do a puzzle but really Heather had to explain what she had seen.

Chapter 8

What Heather saw

After Grandma was out of earshot Heather and Nate began to talk.

"So, Heather, what did you see?" asked Nate, curious and very excited!

"Well, I'm not sure if I actually saw this or if I imagined it because we have had a busy day," Heather began, thinking about what she saw.

"Well…"

"Tell me Heather, what did you see!" blurted Nate, getting more excited by the minute.

Heather took a deep breath.

"Well, Nate, I think I saw a torch light; I'm not sure if it was a torch light or whether it was a candle or something but it was only on for less than a second before it was gone," Heather told her brother.

"Heather are you being serious! This isn't a trick or anything is it?" asked Nate, absolutely flabbergasted.

"Of course not!" Heather said, thinking about what she saw.

"Well, maybe we should go and investigate…" stated Nate, adventurously.

"It could be dangerous, Nate," Heather said to her brother, who was excited by the recent events.

"Well, we'll see," Nate replied, planning in his head to convince Heather that some further investigation was required.

After that, Heather and Nate did a puzzle, they did it in silence as they were tired from their busy and eventful day and also because they were thinking about what Heather had seen from the binoculars that evening... After dinner, Heather and Nate chatted about the topic once more before finally dozing off to sleep.

Chapter 9

A plan for the morning

"Heather, Nate!" called Grandma.

"Are you two awake?"

"Yes, Grandma. Although, Nate is still asleep," smiled Heather.

"Oh ok," Grandma replied.

"Well, this morning I realized that I had ran out of stamps so I need to pop down to the post office to get some more," stated Grandma.

"But I will be away today as I need to give the violin to my friend as she needs it by tomorrow and your Grandpa needs to visit the garden centre as there is a one time only huge discount sale," she sighed.

"So, would you both be alright on your own for a couple of hours?"

"Yes, we should be alright and if we need you, we will telephone you," Heather replied.

"Thank you very much," Grandma said, relieved.

"So, should we go and get some stamps for you from the post office?"

"That would be very useful, yes please."

"Ok, we'll go right after our breakfast," Heather proclaimed, wondering the same thing you probably are...

Will they see the mysterious man once more...?

Chapter 10
Off to the post office once more

When Nate woke up, Heather told Nate th e plan for the day…

"Ok, let's go to the post office soon," Nate said.

"We don't want to go when it's busy," he added .

"Yeah."

"Nate, do you think that we will see that man again?" Heather asked him, knowing that he was probably thinking of the same thing.

"That's what I was thinking too!"

"I hope we do because we can watch him for the whole day to see if he does anything suspicious; because I think he is up to no good," Nate said.

"Nate!"

"We can't just spy on him!"

"Maybe he's just one of those people who we recognise but don't know where from!" Heather announced, wanting to keep out of the business of this man.

"Well, let's just go there and see what happens!" Nate said, mysteriously…

After Heather and Nate had finished their morning routine, they were on their way to the post office...

"Look, we are here," Heather said to her younger brother, who was still walking down the road.

"Oops!" grinned Nate.

They went inside and in the storeroom at the back, they saw that familiar face once more...

"Heather, look," whispered Nate.

The man was putting newspapers into his bag to deliver, this time he was a paper boy! But whilst doing that he was also writing a note...

"What's he writing?" Nate asked Heather.

But Heather just shrugged her shoulders.

"This pen is running out of ink," cursed the man under is breath.

"Now, I must be off, I'll deliver this note after I deliver all the newspapers," he said in a hurry to himself before wheeling his bicycle out of the storeroom and putting the note in his pocket.

Heather and Nate hid behind a bookshelf and then waited before Nate said:

"Heather, get some stamps and then let's follow him."

"Nate, he's going to go all over town to deliver newspapers!"

"But we want to see who that note was for and what it said!" argued Nate.

"Ok, well I have a better idea."

"He's delivering the note last, right?" she asked.

"Yes," replied Nate, puzzled and confused.

"So, who's last to get newspapers delivered to them?"

"Someone with a last name that begins with 'Z'," said Nate.

"So, who's last name begins with 'Z'?" pondered Heather.

"Mr Zak!" remembered Nate.

"So, we go and wait outside Mr Zak's house till the paper boy delivers Mr Zak his newspaper and then we follow him!" announced Heather, proudly.

"Yes, that's a great idea."

"So now we won't get tired running all around town after a man on a bike!" laughed Nate.

"Yes!"

"Now, let's go and buy these stamps," decided Heather.

They paid for the stamps and Heather tucked them safely away in her large coat pocket.

"Now then!"

"Let's go to Mr Zak's house!"

They both walked to Mr Zak's house and hid inside a large hollowed out bush waiting for the paper boy to come.

"Heather are you sure Mr Zak gets papers delivered to his door?" asked Nate.

"I think so, but I'm not one hundred percent sure," Heather replied.

"Because, Grandma and Grandpa don't get their papers delivered to them, they go and collect them," Nate backed up.

"Yes, Nate, but they are both retired so they have time to collect them every week but Mr Zak is young and works," Heather reminded.

"Oh yes."

After an hour of waiting and impatient groaning (mostly coming from Nate!) they finally saw the mysterious man come to deliver his final delivery.

"Nate, come on, let's follow him," commanded Heather.

Stealthily, Heather and Nate followed the man through town…

They never took their eyes off him in case he somehow disappeared! Heather and Nate were very tired as the man was speeding on a bicycle and they were just walking.

"Heather, this is tiring," sighed Nate.

"I wonder where he is going," Heather contemplated.

"We are almost at the end of town!" she added.

Then, Nate gasped.

"Heather, you don't think," he said before pausing.

"That the man is going to the abandoned house, do you?" breathed Nate.

"I hope not."

"If he is, he must be going in there to cover up something dark," Heather gulped.

"You're right."

"If he does go there, we won't follow him in," Heather said quickly.

"Why?" asked Nate.

"Because, we have absolutely no supplies, if there is something going on there, we would need a camera and so on."

"That's true."

"Come on, Nate, we are losing him!" announced Heather.

Soon, Heather and Nate came to the field surrounding the abandoned house…

They hid in a bush and waited to see what would happen next…

"Nate look."

"There's someone sitting on a picnic blanket near the house."

"Oh my! You're right."

"And the man is walking towards her!"

"She seems to be an artist, look, she's painting the landscape that she sees."

"Oh yes."

Heather and Nate held their breath. What was going to happen next?

To their utmost shock, the man gave the lady the note and then walked away!

He wasn't heading into the abandoned house after all!

"Heather, hide," hissed Nate.

They both hid behind a bush and then waited for the man to pass.

"Come on Heather, I want to go and interrogate that artist lady immediately," said Nate.

"Nate, we need a plan, if we are going to do that!" cried Heather.

"Let's pretend we were on a walk and just came across her," decided Nate.

"Nate! Wait! No!" hissed Heather, but Nate was already walking towards the lady.

"Hello," greeted Nate.

Heather ran after her brother, fuming at how careless he was!

What if this person is a criminal? We don't even have a proper plan! Heather said to herself in her head.

"Hello there," Nate said slightly louder as the lady didn't hear.

The lady still did not hear so Nate went and stood very near her before saying 'hello' once more!

"Gracious you gave me a fright!" exclaimed the lady.

She looked up at Nate and then gasped, she gave him the same look that the man had given them both – it was a look that showed they were surprised to see them and that they recognized them but wouldn't say why.

Then there was an awkward silence.

"Hello," Nate repeated.

"Bellow?" misunderstood the artist.

"What ever are you bellowing for?" lisped that lady.

She was middle-aged and had brown hair in a messy bun with streaks of grey coming through; she had lipstick neatly put on her thin lips and powder smothered on her face; she was average height; she was wearing a pair of dungarees that were slightly torn and ripped here and there and inside a pale yellow top with frills on the sleeves; there were flamboyant bracelets and bangles on her wrists and a small chain necklace around her neck.

"I said hello! Not bellow!" clarified Nate.

"Please speak up, I wouldn't say I have the greatest hearing," she informed.

"I said HELLOOOOO!" shouted Nate.

"Oh ok, well hello to you," she replied.

"What on earth are you doing here?" she asked, eyeing the house suspiciously, as if there was something inside that she didn't want Nate to see.

"Well, my sister and I were just on a walk and we happened to walk here," Nate yelled, now that the lady didn't have great hearing!

"Oh, where's your sister?" she asked.

Nate pointed to Heather who was slightly distanced from the artist and Nate.

Heather waved.

"Now, what are your names?" asked the artist.

"We are Heather and Nate," blurted Nate, in his normal voice – forgetting to shout.

"Feather and Grate?"

"What peculiar names you have," laughed the artist.

"We said Heather and Nate!" Shouted Heather.

Then, Nate heard something coming from the abandoned house, it sounded like a click. He turned around and saw a face peeping out from the curtains! Nate gasped; this was a face he knew. Or so he thought. Heather heard Nate gasp and asked:

"Nate are you okay?"

Nate nodded and mouthed: I have something to tell you.

Heather nodded modestly.

"So, you said your names are Heather and Nate; not Feather and Grate."

"Am I right?" asked the artist.

"Yes," mumbled Nate, still in shock after what he had seen.

"Tess?" asked the artist, misunderstanding Nate.

"No, my name is not Tess! My name is Jenny," she said to them.

"Jenny, what are you actually doing here?" asked Nate, firmly.

"What do you mean, Grate?"

"I'm sorry, Nate, not Grate."

"I mean why are you actually here," said Nate.

"Why am I actually deer?"

"Of course, I am not a deer! I am a person!" she announced, offended that anyone could say she looked like a deer.

"My brother said: WHY ARE YOU ACTUALLY HERE?" yelled Heather.

The artists face went a bright shade of crimson red.

"Well, to do painting, and draw the landscape around me," she mumbled; her face filled with trepidation. Are these children on to me? She thought in her head.

"WHAT DO YOU KNOW ABOUT THAT HOUSE?!" asked Nate, loudly – so that she could hear!

"What house?" asked the artist (trying to play dumb).

"That one there," said Heather pointing at the abandoned house.

"Oh, well, umm, hmm, let me see, well, I know that it's abandoned," replied the artist, her voice cracking.

"What else?"

"I know that you are lying," Nate interrogated, menacingly.

"Grate, I do know one thing about that house and that is that you should never enter it or venture too near as it is dangerous," she warned.

"How?" pondered Nate.

"Cow? No, there are certainly no cows inside it!" laughed the artist, hoping that the children would just go away.

"HOW IS IT DANGEROUS?" screamed Heather, getting annoyed with how deaf this lady was.

"Oh, well, you see, there is a family of highly savage foxes who live inside and an army of a thousand bats waiting for someone to attack," she blurted, proud of herself for thinking of (what she thought) was a very good answer.

Nate gave her a cold stare.

"WHAT ARE YOU HIDING JENNY? WHAT ARE YOU UP TO?" asked Heather, menacingly.

"Nothing, nothing at all," she said quietly, her voice quivering.

Heather and Nate both gave her a cold stare and then Nate said:

"Heather we must get going."

"Yes," Heather replied.

"But be warned Jenny, if you are hiding something we will know, and we will soon find out what and why..." warned Nate.

However, Jenny didn't hear this final statement of Nate's, but, someone else did. Someone who Nate had seen in the house, someone who was now worried that the children would interfere with their plans...

Chapter 11

What Nate saw

After they left the field, Heather and Nate began to talk.

"Nate, what was it that you wanted to tell me?" Heather asked.

"Oh yes," whispered Nate.

"Well, you see, Heather."

"I don't know how to put this."

"But."

"Don has escaped from prison," informed Nate, with an anxious look on his face.

"WHAT?!" asked Heather, getting very worried.

Don, was the leader criminal from Heather and Nate's first adventure...

"Well, this is what happened."

"I heard a noise coming from the house, and so looked over there and peeping out from the drawn curtains of the house was Don!" explained Nate.

"Nate are you being serious?" asked Heather, in a very serious voice.

Nate nodded his head.

"Except, remember that scar that Don had on his

cheek?"

"Yes," said Heather, shivering at the mention of Don.

"Well, it was gone," Nate said.

"I didn't see it."

"How is that possible?" pondered Heather.

"I'm not sure."

"But it was definitely Don that I saw," reassured Nate.

"Well, Nate we must get to the police department immediately and tell them what you saw".

"Then, they will call up the prison and see if Don is there or not," planned Heather.

"Ok."

"But what about Grandma and Grandpa?" asked Nate.

"We'll go back to their house first and then we will set off once more," informed Heather.

"Ok, that sounds like a plan."

After a lot of walking, Heather and Nate finally reached their Grandparents' house and then knocked on the door. It was quickly answered.

"Heather, Nate, where on earth have you been?" asked Grandma, in a worried voice.

"We went on a bit of a walk," Heather said, on be-half of both of them.

"Ok," sighed Grandma, relieved that they were okay.

"Oh, and we have got the stamps!" reminded Nate.

"Oh yes," said Heather, before taking the pack of stamps out of her coat pocket.

"Thank you very much," thanked Grandma.

"Now, your lunch is ready on the table," she informed, ushering them inside.

Heather and Nate smiled; Grandma really had made them a feast!

There were cheese and tomato sandwiches; egg sandwiches, pickle sandwiches; a big, fresh, bowl of salad; potatoes smothered in butter and herbs; for dessert there was a big strawberry jelly with vanilla ice cream and some fruit tarts.

Heather and Nate ate happily and when they were done, they told their Grandma that they would go for another quick walk, but really, they were going to the police department…

Chapter 12
The police department

Heather and Nate ran to the police department that was in the North of Oak Town (there was one in the South as well; that's the one that Heather and Nate visited on their last adventure) and soon they arrived. It was a short run to the centre of town and Heather and Nate's hearts were racing.

"We are finally here," sighed Heather when she and Nate reached the police department.

"Now, Nate, tell them exactly what you saw," planned Heather, but Nate had already entered the police department!

Heather and Nate waited in the queue and it was moving very, very slowly! There were people reporting all sorts of things like: a lost cat, super noisy builders that were digging up the road, shops not accepting refunds and some other stuff that Heather and Nate could not hear.

Finally, it was Heather and Nate's turn to speak...

"Hello, Heather and Nate, how can I help you today?" asked PC Jones.

"PC Jones, please can we speak to you in a different room as we don't want anyone else overhearing what we need to say to you," ushered Heather, looking around.

"Oh ok, I'll ask someone to fill in for me here and then you can tell me what has happened," decided PC Jones, before popping off to go and fetch someone to fill in for him. Then, he returned and whisked Heather and Nate away into a small office.

"Now, what did you need to tell me?" asked PC Jones, in a kind voice.

"Well, I think that Don has escaped from prison," breathed Nate, cutting straight to the chase.

"WHAT?!" asked the officer, hoping that he had heard wrong.

"You see, I think I saw him in the abandoned house, near the borders of town," confessed Nate.

"That abandoned house. It has been abandoned for decades!" informed the officer.

"So, if Don escaped prison he would make no business there, he would want to flee from town immediately," added PC Jones.

"But I will definitely make a phone call to the prison right away to ask if Don is still there," reassured PC Jones, going to get a telephone.

"Nate, are you one hundred percent sure that it was Don that you saw?" asked Heather after the officer left the room.

"Well, I think so, I only saw his face for a split second."

"Ok," replied Heather.

Then, PC Jones came back.

"I just called the prison and they said Don is still there," informed PC Jones.

Heather sighed a sigh of relief but Nate was thinking. If it wasn't Don, who was it that he had seen…

Soon, Heather and Nate left the police department and were on their way home.

"I think you must have imagined seeing Don in the window," Heather said to Nate.

"Maybe, but I'm sure that it was him I saw."

"Well, before we left, PC Jones said that it's probably nothing to worry about and that you must have imagined it," Heather reminded.

"Maybe the police should investigate the house," Nate said.

"Nate, they are very busy at the moment, with the case on the counterfeit money makers," Heather said.

"Yeah."

"But Heather, maybe we should explore the house a bit, if there's nothing to hide in there, we would be doing no harm," Nate said.

"Well, maybe we should just make sure there is really nothing going on there," Heather replied, with a twinkle of adventure in her hazel eyes.

"Let's go tomorrow," decided Nate.

"What are we going to tell Grandma and Grandpa?" mused Heather.

"Hmmm, we'll just tell them we are going camping!"

"Besides, it's not like we are getting ourselves into any trouble, PC Jones said so," smiled Nate.

"Yes Nate, but PC Jones also said to keep away and-," began Heather.

"Well, someone has to investigate," interrupted Nate.

"Ok then, Nate."

"But we will leave at the first sign of danger," decided Heather.

"Agreed?"

"Ok, agreed."

Then, they went back home and asked their Grandparents if they could go camping...

To their delight, they said yes! And said that they could leave the very next day!

Heather and Nate were delighted and began to pack and make plan straight away! But little did they know what would happen on this next trip...

Chapter 13

Going to the abandoned house

The following morning, Heather and Nate set off on their camping trip. They planned that: for a couple of hours they would explore the house and then they would enjoy a nice camping trip. Then, they had their breakfast and set off. The weather was warm and cloudy with plenty of shade!

"Gosh, this is exciting!" exclaimed Nate.

"I wonder if we will find something in the house," deliberated Heather.

"Yeah."

"I'm sure that there is something going on in there but yesterday PC Jones told us that nothing will be happening there," Nate restated.

"Yeah."

Heather and Nate thoroughly enjoyed the walk.

"These are the kind of holidays I like; lots of walks and away from crowds of people or busy areas!" smiled Heather.

"Yes, me too."

"Oak Town is the best place to live on the entire world! So many countryside walks and cold lake swims!" Nate listed.

"Yes, imagine wanting to live in a big city when you can live in Oak Town," laughed Heather.

Along the way, they climbed trees, played hide and seek, Nate collected some interestingly shaped pebbles and then they finally reached the small field that surrounded the house.

"Look, that artist isn't there anymore!" said Nate, delighted.

"Nate, it looks like you said that a little too early, look, she's coming over there," pointed Heather.

"Heather, follow me," said Nate, running to the house.

Heather had no time to think, she just ran after Nate. Nate hid in the thick vegetation that immersed the house and soon after, Heather did too.

"Nate, what do you think you are doing?" asked Heather, what if we get seen here.

"Well, that artist will probably sit there for the rest of the day so this is our only shot at getting past her!"

"Fine," sighed Heather.

"Let's watch her to see what she will do next," whispered Nate.

Heather nodded.

They watched her for around fifteen minutes before they decided to find a way into the house.

"Let's see if there are any open windows or holes

in the walls that we can enter through as the front door looks bolted," Heather intended.

They snuck round the house, still hidden by the vegetation that grew all round it. Then, Nate stepped on a stick that gave a very loud *snap*! The artist immediately looked in the direction of the sound. She squinted her eyes and looked in at the vegetation. Heather gave Nate a beseeching look.

"Grate! Is that you again!?" called the artist, before taking a small walkie-talkie out of her dungaree pocket and speaking into it with an ushered voice.

"Well, maybe I was seeing things, it probably isn't Grate, or Feather for that matter!" stated Jenny – the artist.

"Nate, do you think this is a trap?" asked Heather.

"Well, there's only one way to find out if it is," said Nate, daringly.

"Nate, wait!" whispered Heather, but Nate was already making his way around the house and then, he found an entrance.

"Heather, look, here's a hole in the wall!" exclaimed Nate, gesturing towards the hole.

"Nate, I really don't think we should be here, let's go back and maybe we can come here with the police," uttered Heather.

"Well, then, the artist would see us leaving and imprison us," Nate replied.

"Nate! Why did you have to run here!" cursed Heather.

"We knew something was 'up' so we should have told the police to come with us!" regretted Heather.

"Heather, stop thinking about what we should have done!"

"We are here now and we have found an entry so let's explore," Nate instructed.

Heather sighed.

"Well, I suppose we should then," she agreed.

Nate smiled excitedly, wondering what they were going to discover. But Heather smiled anxiously, what were they going to find? She thought.

Chapter 14

Heather and Nate squeezed through the small hole that led into the abandoned house and they discovered that it was the entrance to a passageway...

"Look, Nate, this seems to be a passageway of some sort," observed Heather.

"Oh yeah!"

"Oh dear, Heather, it just seems to get narrower! My large bag won't fit through anymore," Nate said, miserably.

"Oh, that's annoying, in that case mine won't either!" Heather said, wondering what to do next.

"How about we go back into the bush and then take the things we will need out of my bag and put them in the small drawstring bag that contains our pegs and things for the tent," Heather suggested.

"Ok, yes, that sounds like a plan," Nate replied.

Then, they went back into the cave of thick vegetation that engrossed the house and began to take things out of their bags that they thought they would need.

"Camera," whispered Heather, putting into the bag.

"Gloves, to hide our fingerprints," Nate whispered, putting two pairs of gloves in the bag.

"Torch," Heather whispered.

"A few sweets?" questioned Nate, wanting at least some food to keep them going.

Heather nodded, she too wanting at least something to eat because they didn't know how long they would explore the house for.

"Oh yes, and a flask of water!" Heather reminded.

Then, Heather put some string and elastic bands in the bag and then she whispered:

"I think that's everything, are you ready to go back through the passage now?"

Nate nodded, before Heather led the way.

They entered the passageway and instantly an explosion of dust ambushed them as they crawled through.

"Heather, do you think we should switch the torch on so we can see what's ahead of us as this passage seems quite long," Nate pondered.

"Hmm, I'm not sure, someone might see the light, I vote we keep it turned off," Heather replied.

"That's true."

"Wait, Nate, stop crawling," Heather instructed after they both crawled for approximately another few meters or so.

"The passage comes to an end," Heather whispered.

"Ok, is anyone in sight?" Nate asked.

"Not that I can see, I can't hear anyone either," Heather observed.

"Ok."

"Shall we go into the house then, or shall we wait a little bit longer?" asked Nate.

"I'll look into the room and see," Heather decided.

Heather peeped into the room and it was deserted but it was packed full of mess!

"The room's empty but it's absolutely filthy!" she announced.

"Ok, lets leave this cramped passage then!" Nate sighed, glad that they would finally be leaving the dusty passageway!

"Wow, you're right, this room is a mess!"

"But everything is coated in a thick layer of dust and grime, it doesn't look like anyone has been here for a very long time!" Heather stated.

"Yes, but I'm sure that I saw Don in the window, I'm not leaving this place until it is thoroughly searched," Nate said, still adamant that it was Don he saw.

Heather sighed.

"Ok, Nate."

"Oh, my goodness!" shrieked Heather, forgetting to be quiet!

"What is it Heather, what happened? Are you alright?!"

Heather was shocked after what she had seen! Nate was right, someone has been here! She said to herself.

Chapter 15
The orange

"Heather, what happened? Are you alright, you look scared and pale?" Nate comforted.

"I'm alright, it was just something that I saw," Heather replied.

"What is it that you saw Heather?" Nate asked.

Heather pointed.

"What?"

"It's an orange, Nate," Heather said.

Nate gasped.

"So, it is!" he exclaimed.

"And, it's not mouldy!" Heather began.

"So that must mean that someone else is in the house or has visited the house and left this orange here," Nate interrupted.

"Yes," Heather said, slightly worried.

"Nate, we need to get out of this house and head to the police department, then, come back here with some officers," Heather stated.

"Yes, I agree with you Heather, we will come back with officer, but for now let's go!"

Heather and Nate silently crawled back through

the passageway that they came from; but Heather instantly stopped Nate from going much further as Jenny (the artist) was there and she was on the phone with someone.

Heather gestured to Nate, for him to crawl back; they did so and soon found themselves back in the room.

"Heather, what happened? Why did you say we had to come back?" Nate pondered.

"The artist was right outside and she was on the phone with someone," Heather informed.

"Oh," Nate replied.

"Wait here, I will go back through the passage and see who she's talking to and what she's talking about," Nate decided, bravely.

"Ok."

"Wait, before you go, Nate, take the camera with you and take an audio recording of the conversation between her and the person on the phone. It might be useful to show the police or whatnot!" Heather said.

"Sure, Heather, I will do that."

After that, Nate crawled back through the passageway and took an audio recording of what he heard...

Chapter 16
The phone call

"Yes, yes, those children have fallen for the trick of course."

Pause

"Yes, they went through the passage and just left their bags in the bush."

Pause

"Oh really, well I'm by the passage right now so they certainly can't come back out of it."

Pause

"I'll sit by it for the rest of the day as well just to be sure."

Pause

"Yes."

Pause

"Obviously."

Pause

"Anyways, even if they are roaming the house, they will eventually come back to the passage to leave."

Pause

"Yes, I locked all of the windows and doors this

morning, the only one that is unlocked is the one to exit the secret room."

Pause

"I know they are clever; they will never find the entrance to the secret room so we don't need to worry about hiding all the counterfeit money machines."

Pause

"Is he now?"

Pause

"Claude sent me a letter."

Pause

"Yes."

Pause

"He told me that too."

Pause

"So, we are going to send them off to the island - they obviously won't find their way back."

Pause

"Yes."

Pause

They will not be able to escape."

Pause

"Ok."

Pause

"Yes."

Pause

"Yes."

Pause

"I will not take my eyes off the passageway."

Pause

"Alright."

Pause

"Speak to you later."

Pause

"Bye bye Dan," said the artist on the phone.

Nate stopped the audio and then went back to Heather...

Chapter 17

Back to Heather

"What was she talking about?" Heather asked, Nate.

"Well, the counterfeit money machines are in a secret room in this house and the artist was talking to someone called Dan."

"Dan?"

"So not, Don!" Heather stated.

"Yes."

"But he looks like Don so he must be his brother or something," Nate said.

"Oh yes, you're right."

"He must be Don's brother!" Heather said.

Nate nodded.

"Well, here's the bad news, the criminals are planning to capture us and taking us to an island of some sort," Nate informed.

"WHAT!?"

"So, they know we are here in this house and they are planning on capturing us," Heather remarked!

"Yes, so we need to find a way to escape!" Heather exclaimed.

"Yes, we do, but all exits are blocked except for one to exit the secret room and that would be no use to us as we don't know where the secret room is," Nate added.

Heather gulped.

"Nate, we are the only people who can save the town, you do realize that, right?"

"What? How? Why just us?" Nate pondered, mightily confused.

"Well, we are the only people who know that the counterfeit money production is happening in this house so, if we get taken to that island we will not be able to come back to Oak Town and tell the police about what's going on... And, if we ever do get back to Oak Town, the criminals will have probably escaped with all the town's money," Heather lectured.

"Yes, you're right, if we get taken away from the town then the counterfeit money circulation will continue without being stopped," Nate understood.

"Well, if we can't escape the house then we might as well try and find out where that secret room is and then take some photos on the camera; find a printer in the house and print them off; after that, we can write a message on the back of the photos and then throw them out of the house in the hope that someone will alert the police and then come and find us," planned Heather.

"Sounds like a plan."

"But we need to double check that there definitely are no exits because we need to get out of this house and alert the police," Nate reminded.

"Oh yes," Heather replied.

"Well, what are we waiting for! Let's go!"

"Yes, Nate, but we have to be very quiet; and careful," Heather stated.

"Definitely."

Then, they were off…

Chapter 18

Exploring the abandoned house

Heather and Nate crept out of the small, messy room and looked around.

"I'll take pictures of what we see," whispered Nate.

Heather nodded in approval.

"Now Nate."

"There is no point in us both being caught at once so how about you walk a couple of meters behind me if you hear me getting captured then you can run and hide," whispered Heather, planning.

Nate nodded.

"That's a good plan, good job Heather!" Nate whispered, happily.

"Thanks Nate." grinned Heather.

Then, he slipped back a couple of meters behind Heather.

They explored the ground floor and this is what it was like:

The kitchen was slippery with water all over the floor and there were pots and pans carelessly placed here and there and a bin stuffed with rubbish, wrappers and food waste!

"Wow, this room is full of rubbish and food waste!"

Nate remarked.

"Yes, you're right but it's probably because they can't leave the house to empty the bins," replied Heather.

"Oh yeah!"

"That's true," Nate stated, taking some pictures of the messy kitchen.

Then, they left the kitchen and went to the living room...

There were two red sofas that were caked in such a thick coating of dust you could barely tell they were red! There was a TV that was tiny and looked like the kind of thing you would find in an antique shop.

The whole inside of the house was old fashioned for that matter; the wallpaper was brown with age and had old fashioned patterns on it; the carpet was very dusty and unclean, it made Heather and Nate want to be outside in the fresh air. The living room was large and so was the house, but with all the dust, mess, and grime the house looked much smaller than it was. Heather and Nate walked around the living room for some time and then Nate spotted something that was very intriguing; and something that answered one of their most puzzling questions – who are the criminals on the loose?

Chapter 19

The criminals' identities

"Heather, come and look at this!" Nate exclaimed, forgetting to be quiet!

"What is it Nate?" pondered Heather.

"Look," said Nate when Heather reached him.

"Oh, my goodness!" Heather exclaimed!

"They are identity cards!" she added.

"Good job for finding these, Nate," she congratulated, before she began reading the identities of the criminals.

"Look."

"The guy that I thought was Don isn't Don, he's Dan!"

"He must be related to Don in some way though as they have the same last name."

"Oh yes," gulped Heather.

There was silence for a moment as they soon realized who they were up against...

"Heather, I'm scared," mumbled Nate.

Heather hugged her scared younger brother and said that they would find a way out of this but really, she wasn't as confident as she put on to be...

"Let's look at the other identity cards," she said, changing the subject of the rather intimidating Dan.

Then, Heather and Nate let out a massive gasp when they saw who was next… It was the mysterious man!

"This is why we recognized him!" Heather understood.

Her face was a shade of crimson red and she was exploding with so many emotions – rage, shock and worry, she was scared. Nate felt the same, he had butterflies in his stomach.

This was all because the mysterious man was…

Claude Bernard!

Claude Bernard or as you may remember him: PC Bernard was the police officer who didn't believe Heather and Nate last year when they were on the case of the stolen goods and he banned them from the police department!

"Nate, this is PC Bernard that we are up against here!" gulped Heather, her voice quivering in fear and trepidation…

Nate nodded; he was petrified. First, they found out that Don's brother was on the loose and Claude Bernard was working with him!

Heather and Nate stood in silence for a minute or so, taking everything in. After that they proceeded to the third and final identity card.

"Let's look at the final identity card," Heather said, her voice still filled with fear.

"Ok," replied Nate, hoping the final criminal wasn't as bad as the other two…

"Jenny's identity card is all correct," said Nate, reading the name.

Then, they both looked at the photo.

"This is correct as well!" Heather remarked.

Nate scowled.

"I hate her, she calls me Grate!" he added, in a state of annoyance!

"And she calls me Feather!"

"We are on the trail of counterfeit money manufacturing and the criminals are Don's brother, an ex police officer and an artist!" Nate laughed, but it was more of a worried laugh than a happy or funny one…

"Yes, you're right," Heather smiled.

"Nate, take a picture of the identity cards, they might be useful later on," Heather directed.

"Ok."

"Shall we explore another room now?" wondered Nate.

"Yeah, I think we have covered everything that there is to see here."

"I'll lead the way, Nate; you can be a bit further behind in case I get caught or something. Same plan as before," Heather reminded.

Nate nodded, taking some pictures of the room as they left.

Then, they went into a small dining room. It had a large oak dining table that was placed in the middle of the small, cramped room making it hard to navigate around. There were paintings hung on the walls but the canvases were all scratched and dusty so you couldn't see what was painted on them.

The room had a damp and dusty feel to it and Heather and Nate didn't feel like staying for long.

"This room feels so dusty and the air feels unclean," Nate admitted.

"Yeah, it does," Heather replied.

"It's almost like the air is thick and dusty instead of light and clean," Nate said.

"It is because the windows in this house haven't been opened for a long time," she added.

"Yeah."

"Do you want a drink of water, Nate?"

"Yes please, the air also makes me very thirsty!" he replied.

"Yes, it does," Heather realized, handing Nate a small bottle of water before taking one herself.

"Ahh that now feels much better!" Nate remarked,

after having the refreshing drink of water.

"You're right, it does!" Heather agreed.

"You know, this dusty house makes me want to go for a swim!" exclaimed Heather, laughing.

"Yes, so it does!" laughed Nate.

They wandered around the room for some time and then they realized there was nothing there that was useful to them so they left and went on to the next room. It was a bathroom but they soon left as it was minuscule and had absolutely nothing useful inside.

"Now, there's only the library left on the ground floor and I'm guessing more stuff upstairs," Heather said, when they reached the large open space where the doors that led to the rooms of the house all came from... When you entered the house from the front door the first thing you would see would be the stairs around a couple of meters in front of you and on both walls, there would be doors leading off into different rooms...

"Heather, I think we should go upstairs before we go into the library because I assume that all the books will be coated in dust and hopefully the upstairs is less dusty," Nate suggested.

"Ok, sure, let's explore upstairs before we come back down," proclaimed Heather.

Heather and Nate quietly crept up the spiralling staircase but the stairs were creaky with the age and being quiet wasn't that easy! Once they finally reached the landing, at the top of the stairs there were three doors and then a ladder up to the attic… Heather and Nate explored the three doors that led to bedrooms and there was also one bathroom. Heather and Nate spent some time thoroughly exploring all rooms and then they went up the ladder into the attic. The attic looked fairly normal from first glance but it was packed with boxes from floor to ceiling and all boxes were sealed making it a bit mysterious…

"Why are all these boxes sealed?" pondered Heather.

"That was just what I was thinking!" Nate related!

"Hmm."

"Maybe we should open a box or something so see as it is very suspicious," Heather said, wondering what were in the boxes.

"Yes, let's."

They both soon found a pair of scissors in the kitchen and then they raced back up to the attic.

Nate took the scissors and then he slit the cardboard so they could see what was in the boxes…

Then, they opened the boxes and their eyes lit up…

Chapter 20

What was in the box

Heather and Nate opened the box and they were shocked! Inside was wads of money! Enough to make you a very rich person instantly! Nate took out his camera and took some pictures before they both shut the box.

"Wow."

"That money looks very real, but we know that it's counterfeit," Heather breathed.

"Yes, it did look very real, no wonder the townsfolk can't tell that it's counterfeit," Nate responded.

"So, what's going on is the criminals are making counterfeit money and somehow spreading them into Oak Town and in the process, swapping them for the real money meaning they are getting money while making the town poor in the process," Heather began.

"Yes."

"And for example, if someone wanted to take an amount of money from their bank account, they could potentially be taking out counterfeit money and the criminals take the real money," Heather added.

"And, the counterfeit money will be going to the

bank and the bank will need to give it to shops and other places and people in town," she added.

"Yes, you're right," Nate said.

"And we are the only people who can stop this," Nate added, pressurising them.

"I wish there was a way out of this house," Nate wished.

"Me too," Heather said.

"But we have been into every room except for the library now and we have checked and all the windows are locked and bolted!" she added.

"Yeah."

"Shall we open another box?" asked Nate.

"Okay," Heather responded.

Then, they made a slit in another box, made it bigger with their fingers and then, peeped inside.

Heather and Nate gasped.

"In this box there is even more money!" Heather gasped, looking at the wads of money.

They shone in the box and looked so real.

"You mean counterfeit money," corrected Nate.

"Oh yes."

"Counterfeit money," she said to herself.

"There must be so much in here," Nate observed, looking into the box once more.

"Yeah, and they would make an absolute fortune, swapping this for real money," Heather informed.

"These criminals really are sneaky!" said Nate, annoyed at why they would want to do something like that to Oak Town.

"Somehow they are swapping the real money in banks for these fake ones! I wonder how?" thought Nate.

"Heather, I think we should open a couple more boxes and then go to the library downstairs," Nate planned.

"Yes, let's do that."

The next box they opened was filled with more money and they rested their case – there was money in all the boxes…

"Heather, how can we be sure that this is the fake money, for all we know they could be the real wads of cash," Nate realized.

"Oh yes, for all we know these could be the stolen money!" Heather said.

"Hmm."

"Wait, Nate, what's this?" pondered Heather as she picked up a piece of paper that was on the floor.

Heather read the note and then showed Nate, this is what the note looked like:

To, Jenny and Dan,

Here is all the counterfeit money. Look after the loot. We will continue to spread the money.

After the final batch of counterfeit money is spread and the real money is with us, we will flee so that the police can't catch us – hopefully we will be ready to flee by mid this month...

We will leave from Oak Town and escape on a boat through the large river that separates Elm Town, then we will reach open waters (the ocean) and we can go off to our island (where the children will be imprisoned); we will collect them and drop them off back at Oak Town and then we will flee to another country with all the money.

- Claude Bernard

"Wow, I can't believe this is their plan!" exclaimed Nate, after he finished reading the note.

"I know what you mean," Heather replied.

"So, they are planning on escaping across the ocean," Nate announced.

"Precisely, and we can't let them get away with it," Heather said, grimly, thinking of the consequences that Oak Town would face otherwise.

"Once they are out on open water or the sea, they will be impossible to hunt down and find!" Nate sighed.

"Yeah."

There was silence for a moment…

"Should we go and explore the library now, Nate?"

"Yes, let's do that."

They crept down the stairs and they creaked and made loud noises when they were stepped on.

"This is a very loud staircase!" whispered Heather.

"Yeah."

After what felt like an hour of creeping down the stairs Heather and Nate finally reached the door to the library.

They took a deep breath before entering. To their surprise, it wasn't as dusty as they thought it would be!

"I was expecting this room to be dustier as it is a library; it's full of books and old books are very very dusty!" Heather said.

"Yeah, I thought that as well!" Nate pondered.

After that, Heather and Nate paced around the library looking for anything that may be useful to them or maybe even the entrance to that secret room that Jenny was talking to Dan on the phone about.

"If we find the secret room, we will have a chance of escaping as Jenny said the only way to exit the house is through the secret room," Nate stated.

"Yes, you're right, what we really need right now is to find the secret room," Heather replied.

After searching the library thoroughly for around one hour, Heather and Nate gave up...

"I don't think we will find the secret room after all," sighed Nate.

"I hate to say it: but, no, I don't think we will," Heather responded.

"Well, we have searched the whole house so we have no where else to search," Nate said.

"Yeah."

"Maybe we should just stay in this room for a bit because it is the least dusty," suggested Nate.

"Yeah ok, let's do that."

Heather sat down in a large Oak Armchair that had a scarlet red, cushioning and Nate perched on a small blue version. After that, Nate casually walked over to the large, towering bookshelves that spread themselves around three of the four walls in the large, airy, room.

"Heather look at this!"

"What is it?"

"Come and see!"

Heather got up and strode over to Nate.

"What is it, Nate?" she pondered.

"Look," said Nate, before pointing at a large leather bound book.

The book was clearly very old and was a gorgeous

shade of emerald green; the pages were yellow with age yet beautiful in their own way; the book was titled: **Stories of Oak Town**

Heather smiled when she saw the book.

"This is the book we used to love when we were younger!" she exclaimed, happily.

"Yeah, Mum and Dad used to read us a different story every day!" Nate reminded.

Heather smiled.

"I remember you used to love the story about the treasure in the North woods!" Heather remembered.

"Oh yeah!"

"And you adored the story about the secret passageway under the ocean!" Nate laughed, remembering all the stories that they loved.

Heather grinned.

"I wonder if the stories in the book are actually true," pondered Nate.

"Nate! Of course, they are! They have been told for generations and generations and have come from the people who they were about!" Heather said to Nate.

"Yeah, I know, Heather!"

"I was only joking!" laughed Nate.

Heather grinned, shaking her head.

"I still can't believe that we were part of Oak Town's history!" Heather exclaimed, thinking back to last year.

"Yeah, me neither!" Nate exclaimed.

"I wonder if someday our story will be in the book of Stories of Oak Town," pondered Heather.

"I have never thought of it like that, imagine if it will be!" wondered Nate, his eyes shining.

"After all, it's very similar to the Old Story of Oak Town!" Heather announced.

"Almost!" emphasized Nate.

"In the old story of Oak Town, the thieves were never caught so they got away with all the stolen goods but we captured the thieves and then all the goods were returned!" He added, thinking back to their adventure.

"How about to pass time a little we read some stories from the book," suggested Heather.

"Ok!"

After that, Heather slowly yet carefully pulled the beautiful old book from the shelf…

They both looked at the book for a moment before a loud monotonous rumble echoed through the house.

Heather and Nate clutched one another in fear and shock!

"What's that sound?!" cried Nate, surprised by the sudden sound.

"I have no idea!" Heather replied, her voice filled with fear.

The sound rumbled on for some time before it came to an abrupt stop and a section of the book-shelves slid away revealing a dark, dingy passage-way...

Heather and Nate looked at each other and they both knew what they had come across...!

Chapter 21

The secret passageway to the secret room

"It's a secret passageway!" they both said in unison, looking at the passageway and then back at each other.

"This must lead to the secret room!" exclaimed Heather, bubbling with so many emotions: fear, hope, excitement and bravery!

"Yeah!" exclaimed Nate, he too was bubbling with so many emotions: adventure, fright, happiness (that they found the entrance to the passageway) and excitement as to what the adventure will bring!

"Shall we go in?" Nate said, knowing the answer!

"Yeah!"

"Let's go!" Heather exclaimed.

They crept through the passageway and soon it was so dark they couldn't even see each other!

"I'll get the torch out of our bag," Heather said, taking the small red bag off her back and then pulling the torch out of it.

Heather switched the torch on and it illuminated the passageway! They now had a proper look at it, the walls were rock and were coarse and rough. The floor was cobbled with stone and had smooth surfaces and rigid ones balancing each other out.

After a while, Heather gasped and flashed her torch at the floor.

"What is it, Heather?" pondered Nate.

"Look, there is a trail of oil on the floor," Heather began.

"So, someone must have come here recently with an oil lamp," Nate interrupted.

"Yeah, precisely that," Heather said.

"Nate, we might be walking right into the lion's den," Heather said, grimly.

"What do you mean?" asked Nate, slightly confused.

"What I mean is that the criminals will probably be in the secret room at the end of this passageway so we could potentially be putting ourselves at risk by coming here," Heather said, wisely.

"You're right, but we are prisoners in this house right now so it's better to take the risk and at least take a photo of their machines making the counterfeit money and there is the exit in the secret room, so, it is our only way of getting out," Nate informed.

"That's very true," Heather agreed.

After walking a couple more meters, the passageway ended abruptly and a steep staircase going down took over.

"Be careful, Nate, this staircase is very steep and it's dark," Heather warned.

"Oh ok."

"Thank you, Heather!"

They both went down the steep set of stairs and held on to the banister so they didn't stumble forwards. Once they reached the bottom of the staircase the passageway continued and Heather and Nate both cautiously crept through it. Heather decided it would be best to switch the torch off for some time, this way they wouldn't be seen as easily. The passage spiralled under the ground for a long time and then soon it slowly but certainly began opening out – the walls and ceiling were expanding out and it was getting slightly less dark. Then, Heather and Nate heard something that made them stop in their tracks...

Chapter 22

The voices

Heather and Nate stopped in their tracks and listened. They heard voices. It wasn't exactly clear what they were talking about or saying but they were there.

"That's the voice of Dan," Heather snarled, angrily.

"And he's talking to Claude B," Nate added, he too snarling.

Heather and Nate were so angry that the criminals were doing what they were doing to their beloved Oak Town. Heather and Nate loved their town; they loved every bit of it from the rolling hills bordering it from Maple town and the lakes and rivers bordering it from Elm Town and they loved all the townsfolk, cottages, houses, schools (even though there are only two (one primary and one secondary)) but they love the Oak trees the most…

Heather and Nate tried to listen to the conversation that was going on between the two gang members but it was so muffled that they couldn't hear a single word clearly. Nate crept a little further through the passageway and then discovered that there was a large, old, solid oak door! He went back to Heather and then told her what he had discovered.

"Oh my!"

"A large door!" Heather exclaimed.

"Yep," Nate replied.

"Well, Nate, how about we wait somewhere in this passageway until the criminals leave the room and then we go in and do some exploring?" pondered Heather.

"Ok."

"But I doubt that there is anywhere to hide," sighed Nate.

"And I don't particularly want to go all the way back up to the library to hide there," he added.

"Yeah, we shouldn't go back into the library because then, when we want to get back down into the room then we will have to use the book entrance and it makes a lot of noise," Heather agreed.

Heather flashed the torch around the passageway and instantly the dark, dingy passageway was illuminated! The warm light shone all around the cobbled walls and then it shone up on a large niche in the wall.

"Look, Nate, there's a niche in that wall over there," said Heather, before pointing at the wall.

"Oh yes."

"Let's go and crouch in there!" Nate exclaimed.

A niche is basically an alcove or a compartment in a wall; it is usually or more commonly used to display items (paintings, flower vases, etc...)

Heather and Nate crouched in the niche and they felt partly concealed as the niche was quite large! So, they could only be spotted if a torch light was shone on them.

"How long do you think we will have to wait in this niche for, Heather?" pondered Nate.

"I'm not sure, but I will be willing to stay in here as long as we can if it means we can go into the secret room and escaping this house," Heather replied.

"Yes, that's true."

"Jenny said that we will be able to escape from the secret room and if we escape then we can save Oak Town," Nate added.

Heather and Nate hid in the niche for around another twenty minutes before the criminals finally made their way out of the secret room. Then, the criminals began to talk.

"So, I wonder where in the house those interfering little children are?" snarled Dan.

"Well, we know they are somewhere in the house so once we get them, they will be sent off to our island," Claude B said.

"Oh yes," Dan said, grinning menacingly.

"So, after the final counterfeit batch of money is sent into Oak Town and we get the real money and we will flee through the river of Elm Town and then travel to a far away land; and we will have a fortune!" Claude B said, a sly grin on his face.

Dan smirked.

"You seem happy about that, Claude," Dan said to him.

"Well, why wouldn't I be?!" Claude responded, rather defensively.

"I don't know," shrugged Dan.

"Dan, you don't understand how much this whole scheme means to me," Claude said to him.

"Claude, you keep saying that to me! Why does this mean so much to you?!"

"Well, the Oak Town police department fired me because I didn't believe two little children and didn't help them when they thought they were on to something!" Claude said, snarling, angrily.

"Yeah, well being a good police officer is in your past, now you are a criminal," Dan reminded, frustrated with Claude's annoying statements.

"I understand that you want revenge on Oak Town, well, so do I," Dan said, trying not to lose his temper.

"Oak Town put my brother in jail and that's why I want revenge while you just want it because they fired you," sighed Dan, rolling his eyes.

Claude rolled his eyes back at Dan, before scowling, he hated to be embarrassed.

"Well, Claude, we will soon both have what we want (revenge) and on top of that we will have money," Dan said, imagining it all in his head.

Claude B smiled, but it was an evil smile…

"That would be nice," he spoke.

"And there is nothing Heather and Nate would be able to do about it," Claude said, relieved.

"Yes, exactly."

"I'm glad you told me when you found out that they were onto us," Dan said, patting Claude on the back.

Claude nodded proudly, he is self obsessed and feels very very proud when he is praised…

"So, back to the subject of Heather and Nate…" Dan began.

"You said that last night you went to the island to put loads and loads of food there for them?" Dan asked.

"Yes, there is a whole cave of food and other supplies."

"There will be enough there to last them a month or so," he spoke.

"Good."

"And soon after that, we will send them back to their family but by then there will be nothing Oak Town can do to stop us," Dan added.

Claude nodded, trying to keep up with what Dan said.

After that, the criminals began to walk away and their voices and conversation faded. Once they were definitely out of earshot and probably back in the house Heather and Nate looked at one another...

Then, Nate smiled, then giggled, and soon after he laughed... Heather was just puzzled!

Chapter 23
What Nate did

Heather looked at her brother and was puzzled.

"Nate!"

"What is it?!" Heather pondered.

She was trying to think why Nate was smiling and laughing in a moment like this!

"Nate, we just found out what the criminals are planning to do to us!"

"Why are you happy?!" Heather exclaimed, extremely confused by her brother.

"Well, Heather," began Nate, but he couldn't stop smiling!

"Nate!" Heather exclaimed.

Then, Nate pulled the camera out of his pocket. At first, Heather was very confused but then she soon caught on what Nate had done and she too smiled.

"You did it, didn't you!" Heather exclaimed.

"Yes, I did!" Nate exclaimed.

Nate took a recording of the criminals' conversation!

"Now, that's more proof to give the police but what we really need is to get into that secret room and take some pictures of the machines that they are using to make the counterfeit money or whatever else is in there – and then leave!" Heather said, patting her brother on the back!

"Yes, we do," Nate agreed.

"But, very well done Nate!"

"Taking an audio of the criminals' conversation was a great idea!" Heather congratulated.

"Thanks Heather!" beamed Nate.

Heather and Nate listened to the audio of the conversation on the lowest volume (just to be safe!). To their delight, the audio was very clear and it was just the proof that they needed!

"Nate, should we try and get into that secret room now?" asked Heather.

"Yes, let's do that."

Heather and Nate slid out of the niche and stretched their legs.

"Wow, my legs really are cramped!" Nate said, after they left the niche!

"Yeah, same here!" Heather said, stretching her legs.

Then, they both crept through the passageway and headed to the large oak door that guarded the secrets that were locked away in the secret room…

Chapter 24

Into the secret room

Heather and Nate soon arrived at the door and they took a deep breath before Heather put her hand to the door handle and twisted the cold, brass, doorknob... To their delight, the door wasn't locked!

"Yay! The door isn't locked!" exclaimed Heather, a part of her thinking that it would be.

"Yes, it's not!" Nate exclaimed, also very happy.

Then, they both opened the door and peered in...

They both gasped in shock! They were so surprised that for a moment they had totally forgotten where they were and what they were seeing.

"Are you seeing what I see?!" asked Nate, his eyes wide and his mouth even more so!

Heather nodded – too taken aback to talk!

They stared into the room for at least another five minutes before they snapped out of the trance of awe that they were locked in!

"Come on, Nate, let's go in!" Heather exclaimed.

"Oh yes! That's what we are here for!" Nate said, still taken aback by what they had just seen!

This is what they had both seen when they looked

into the room: the room was larger than they expected, it was about the size of a large classroom! The walls were covered in shelves and the shelves were covered with boxes! It was so full that you couldn't see the wall; the room was very neat and organized; but what surprised Heather and Nate most was the three large machines that towered tall and stood proud in the middle of the room; they stretched from the floor to the ceiling and the machines were making something... Heather and Nate assumed that they were manufacturing the counterfeit money.

"These must be the machines that make the counterfeit money!" Nate exclaimed.

"Yeah," Heather replied, looking at the large and slightly intimidating machines!

"Nate, can you take some pictures?" Heather said to her younger brother, who was looking at some boxes on the shelves.

"Oh yes."

"I'll do that!" Nate exclaimed.

Then, Nate took the camera off of the band that it hung from around his neck and started snapping away, taking loads of pictures! After that, they began poking around in the boxes... There were a load of cogs for the machines; they discovered that if you replaced the cogs in the boxes with the cogs in a particular machine then you can manufacture different notes of money! Like, twenty pound notes instead of ten!

"Wow, this machine is amazing," Nate declared after they found out what it did.

"Yes, but it is doing very bad things and that certainly is not amazing!" Heather said.

"Yeah, obviously!" Nate said.

"Isn't it strange how the criminals are putting all their eggs into one basket," Heather stated.

"What do you mean, Heather?" wondered Nate, confused!

"Well, in out last adventure the criminals' base was the tumble down castle and they had all the goods that they stole in the secret shipwreck in the lake," Heather began to explain…

"Oh yes," Nate interrupted.

"I understand now!" he said, realizing what Heather meant.

"So, you mean that these criminals have done everything in the abandoned house; from making the counterfeit money to storing the real ones and even hiding here themselves! So, if the house gets investigated or explored – so basically what we are doing – then Jenny, Claude and Dan's secrets will be out! And also, they will be more vulnerable to the police and stuff like that: which is good for us!" Nate stated.

"Precisely!" Heather exclaimed, patting Nate on

the back.

They carried on exploring for a bit and then, after ten minutes or so, Heather said:

"Nate, I think that now we have got all the pictures and information that we need and we should find that exit and get out of here as soon as possible!" Heather said, ushering them out of the secret room.

"Ok, the sooner we get out of here, the sooner we can tell the police and then the town will be safe," Nate informed, looking around, still taking pictures.

"Look."

"Nate!"

"There's the back door!" exclaimed Heather, eyeing the door.

"Oh yes."

"Now, let's go!" Nate proclaimed, before putting the camera safely away in Heather's bag.

They raced up a steep set of stairs; then opened a door at the top but what they saw as soon as they exited the room was something that shocked them and made them absolutely petrified!

Chapter 25

Captured and taken away

Heather and Nate stepped back in fear and then Nate clung onto Heather and Heather clung onto Nate! There in front of them were Dan, Claude and Jenny! They had smug grins on their faces and Dan and Claude were holding ropes: presumably to tie Heather and Nate's hands together...

"Well, well, well, look who we have stumbled into," snarled Dan, knowing Heather and Nate were there and taken by no surprise that they had stumbled into them!

"It's Feather and Grate!" exclaimed Jenny!

"Come here and give your dear friend, Jenny a hug!" Jenny said, looking at them and tilting her head.

Nate looked at her and rolled his eyes!

"Grate! That's very rude!" Jenny exclaimed, telling Nate off!

"Anyways!" interrupted Dan.

"You silly, interfering children have seen enough," Claude butted in.

"Claude, I was about to say that! That was my line!" Dan scowled.

"Where was your wine? I want wine!" Jenny said, getting giddy.

"Silence," commanded Dan.

"Pie fence!"

"That sounds peculiar!" Jenny announced.

Everyone rolled their eyes at Jenny and she looked at them confused.

"Well, did you think we didn't know that you were in our house?!" Claude asked, laughing in glee that they had captured Heather and Nate.

"Umm."

"Well."

Heather and Nate said, not knowing what to say to Claude's remark.

"Exactly, you have nothing to say," Claude smirked, trying to sound smarter than he was.

"That's enough, Claude," shushed Dan.

Claude nodded, embarrassed, he was always trying to impress his boss (Dan) but he always ended up overdoing it!

"Well, you two are coming with us, as you have seen too much! All will be explained soon..." Dan told them, glowing with pride that he and his gang had captured Heather and Nate! Dan did not know that Heather and Nate had heard his conversation with Claude or his and Jenny's phone call – so, he thought they knew nothing about the criminals' plan.

"Where are we going?" Heather asked them.

"Hair are we snowing?" asked Jenny.

"Ah you must mean," began Jenny before pausing dramatically!

Everyone looked at her hoping that she would say what Heather had actually said! But she disappointed them by saying:

"Is it snowing hair?" she finished.

"The answer is no; it is not snowing hair! Although I wonder where I can go to see it snowing hair. Has anyone got any suggestions?" pondered Jenny, as hilarious as ever but Heather and Nate weren't in the mood for laughs…

They were petrified for what would happen to them and they were petrified that no one even knew that they were missing as their Grandparents thought that they were going on a camping trip!

This is the second adventure that has started through a camping trip! Heather said to herself in her head.

After an awkward pause Dan whispered to Claude B:

"Tie their hands up."

Then, swiftly Claude B tied the rough rope around Heather and Nate's hands and he tied it EXTRA tight making the rope burn into their wrists and make them sore…

"Ouch! This is tight!" Nate shrieked.

"Yes, it is!" Heather screeched!

"Tess it is! Goodness gracious me, I have told you before, Feather and Grate, my name is not Tess!" Jenny said, rather strictly!

The mood was tense but the misinterpretations of sentences that Jenny muddled up was hilarious!

"Let's go now," Claude said to Dan.

"It's getting dark," he added.

"I'm getting bark!?" Jenny exclaimed.

"I'm not sure why you need bark at this time of day, Claude; but you go and do that, get some bark," Jenny stated, looking around to see if there were any trees near by that would be good to collect bark from!

"Look, that tree over there has loads of bark on the ground around it! Go and get your bark from there, Claude," Jenny recommended; she was acting as if it was very useful information as she pointed into the woods, so, you couldn't really tell which tree she was talking about.

After this remark that she made no one bothered to reply; although, Heather and Nate felt like laughing! Jenny was just as eccentric as Barry (Barry was a hilarious criminal from Heather and Nate's previous adventure)!

"Yes, Claude, you're right IT'S GETTING DARK, we best make a move on," Dan said, emphasizing the part that Jenny mixed up!

Soon, Heather and Nate's ankles were tied together and a blindfold was loosely tied over their eyes as well; then they were put into a wagon and they were pulled away...

Heather and Nate were pulled through the countryside and soon, they reached a car...

Nate of course couldn't see the car, but he could definitely hear it.

"Wow, these criminals are serious, they have a car!" Nate whispered to Heather, as cars were quite a rare sight in Oak Town!

They were loaded into the large boot of it and all the windows were open halfway so that they could have ventilation... Before they knew it, they were being driven away.

"So, Heather and Nate, we will be escorting you two to an island," Dan informed, calmer than he felt and the calm tone made Heather and Nate want to shout: WHY ARE YOU SO CALM YOU ARE KIDNAPPING US!

Heather and Nate just nodded, as they couldn't think of what to say to this remark.

"You will stay on the island until we are done doing what we are doing and flee from Oak Town..."

"There are loads of supplies there for you like food and blankets and other essentials," Jenny said, grinning broadly for some reason, although, Heather and Nate couldn't see that as they were blindfolded.

"Yes," Claude contributed.

"So, after we flee, we will come back to collect you from the island and then send you back to your family" Dan snarled, pleased that their plan was going so well.

"And how long will it take for you to flee, then come and drop us back off at home?" Nate asked, hoping he would say one day or something small but deep down he felt as if it would be months.

"Around a couple of months or so," Dan said calmly, smirking.

"A couple of months!" Nate exclaimed, heavily frustrated.

"Don't worry! It will be like a lovely holiday!" Jenny replied.

"I am sure that you will love it, Grate," she added.

Nate scowled but said nothing.

Everyone rolled their eyes at her.

The car chugged through Oak town for around another fifteen minutes – but to Heather and Nate it felt like fifteen hours... After the car stopped the boot was opened and Heather and Nate were carelessly pulled out of it and then dropped to the hard, grassy ground. As it was dark the only light that they had was moonlight and it was very hard to see – not that Heather and Nate could! The large pale moon shone proudly in the deep midnight sky and even though it was only eight o'clock it was dark and eery...

"Claude, carry the boy," Dan commanded, before firmly holding Heather and dragging away from the car.

Soon, they were in the woods... Once they were under the cover of darkness, Heather and Nate's blindfolds were slipped off and they could see once more. They were stumbling through the woods in the dark and then Heather and Nate heard water... At first it was just drops plipping and plopping and then it became a trickle and slowly but surely it became a splashing river! It was the river of Elm Town!

Elm Town is a very small town that neighbours Oak Town; Elm Town has two sides to it, and those sides are split by a river... The river runs through Elm Town and there's not a place where it stops for the sides of the Town to come together. The river is long and wide, it is probably as wide as a tall tree turned on it's side... The river eventually runs into the ocean as Elm Town is a town on the coast...

"We are at the river of Elm Town!" Heather whispered to Nate.

"We are at the silver of elm gown!" misunderstood Jenny, looking around for a gown!

Jenny was priceless!

Soon, Heather and Nate were boarded onto a small rowing boat. There were sacks put over their heads so that no one would recognise them and there were eye holes cut out so that they could see and a hole near their mouths so that they could breathe. Dan rowed the boat strongly, Heather and Nate watched the crystal clear water lap around the oar as it cleanly sliced through the water, it was mesmerising and enthralling yet they felt obliged to look ahead to see where the boat was heading. They couldn't see very far ahead of them, and soon they could see nothing at all as the moon was concealed by a large dark cloud. Jenny had a torch so she switched it on, but she was waving the light around wildly trying to find that silver gown made out of elm!

Heather giggled.

Nate laughed.

"What's so funny?" she asked, genuinely confused!

Dan smiled before quickly restoring a straight face and Claude let out a small peal of laughter but turned it into a cough.

Soon, the boat came to the end of the river and the river opened out into an ocean... Heather and Nate looked around and then they saw how they were going to be getting across the ocean… There towering in front of them was a large pirate ship! It had a large, dark oak deck and an array of grimy circular windows that were on the bottom deck of the ship; the mast was tall and strong and the flag was crisp white and had a black ship on it – exactly the same as the one that stood in front of them! Heather and Nate's eyes darted around the towering ship; it was amazing! They had never seen anything like it in their entire lives.

"Wow," gaped Heather, in awe.

"This is amazing!" Nate shrieked, his eyes darting across the ship.

"There's no time to waste you silly children!" Claude roared.

"Claude is right – for once!"

"Let's get moving!" Dan declared.

Heather and Nate were shoved towards the ship and then Jenny pressed a button that released a ladder.

"Go on then, climb up!" she said, pointing at the ladder.

"We can't, you guys tied our legs and hands up!" Nate reminded, getting slightly annoyed.

"Oh yes," Dan said, pondering how to get Heather and Nate up into the ship."

"Claude, untie their legs for a minute," Dan commanded.

"And don't let them go anywhere but up the ship!" He added.

First, Claude untied Heather's legs and made her climb up the ladder. It was hard for her as her hands were still tied to together but eventually, she was in!

"One down two to go!" Jenny exclaimed.

Everyone looked at Jenny, to see if she was joking but she just looked back at them all, blankly.

"What?" she asked eventually, growing curious at why everyone was looking at her!

"Jenny, you said: one down two to go!" Dan told her, hoping she'd correct her mistake, but she just looked at him even more blankly.

Dan sighed and rolled his eyes.

"You mean to say: one down one to go!" Dan corrected.

"What?" Jenny asked.

"One town one flew home?!" Jenny said, looking at them all.

"I never knew towns could fly!" she announced, rather enthusiastically.

"Has Oak Town ever flown?" she asked them all curiously.

No one knew what to say and no one could be

bothered to correct her for about the millionth time that day!

"Claude, get Nate up and then we can make a move on," Dan sighed.

"Ok."

Soon, Nate too was swiftly up onto the boat and Heather and Nate were escorted down to a cabin under the deck. They were asked to stay there with Claude B as Jenny could not be trusted and Dan was the strongest so he had to steer the boat and guide it in the right direction! The calm ocean did not move at all as the vast ship smoothly sailed through. The water was crystal clear; there were schools of fish in colours Heather and Nate didn't even know existed! Blue, green and silver all mixed into one! Orange, red and gold! Purple, blue and bronze! They watched in awe. They could see the most amazing things from the cabin of the boat!

Claude B watched the children like an eagle eyeing prey. He took his role very seriously as he was always trying his absolute best to impress Dan... The ship calmly glided across the waters; barely making a sound.

"This island seems far away!" Heather quietly hissed to Nate.

Claude's sharp ears heard the whisper and eyed them coldly.

"It's only four kilometres you foolish children!"

Claude said, giving them cold stares.

Nate nodded.

They both then looked out of the window that was in the cabin and their eyes lit up…

Chapter 26
The island is in sight

"The island!" Heather and Nate exclaimed in unison, forgetting that they had to be quiet as Claude was there!

"SILENCE!" commanded Claude.

"Silly children!" he muttered under his breath.

Heather and Nate scowled – they hated to be called silly! The ship sailed closer and closer to the island and they could see it better now. There was a small stone cottage that was half in ruins; by the looks of it a little beach and harbour for boats and a cove! Heather and Nate felt loads of different emotions: part of them was excited to explore the island but the larger part of them was extremely worried, not just for themselves but also for their Parents and Grandparents...

Soon, the ship came to halt in the harbour and it was time for Heather and Nate to get off. Claude quickly ushered both of them up onto the deck and then Dan lead them off of the ship (whilst making sure they didn't try and run back on board) and to make things slightly awkward Jenny was crying and giving them an emotional farewell. Heather and Nate were half wondering why Dan had actually hired Jenny! After they were on the small beach, Dan said:

"The food is in the cave and so are your rooms!"

"See you never again!" he smirked, beaming at how smoothly his plan had worked out!

"Ha-ha!" laughed Claude!

"See you never!" he cried, copying Dan.

"But Dan, we will see them when we come back to take them home to Oak Town," reminded Claude.

Dan scowled, he hated how Claude ruined his moment of victory.

"See you lever?" pondered Jenny. Then, she frantically looked around before she noticed that there was a lever next to the wheel that Dan used to guide the ship and she pulled it. To her surprise the boat shook before speeding off abnormally fast with Dan, Claude and herself screaming. Heather and Nate watched them until they were out of sight and then they looked at one another.

"This is one very cool island!" Nate commented, trying to cheer Heather up, but she was very worried and she was deep in thought.

Nate noticed that she was thinking about something. And said:

"Heather, what are you thinking about?" he pondered.

"Well, it's just that I have a theory..." Heather began.

"What is it?!" asked Nate, very intrigued.

"Nate, do you remember that story about the island from the book: Stories of Oak Town?" Heather asked Nate, looking at him, hoping that he would remember.

"What?" questioned Nate, looking at Heather, puzzled, racking his brain trying to think about what Heather was talking about.

"Nate!"

"The story about the secret passageway under the ocean!" She blurted out.

"Oh yes!"

"I remember!" Nate exclaimed, remembering that story about the secret passageway.

"You mean the one about the passageway that leads from a long lost island to Oak Town!" Nate said, jumping up and down!

"Yes!"

"Precisely!" Heather proclaimed.

"So, my theory is that the long lost island is actually this island and that there is a secret passageway from here back to Oak Town!" Heather worked out, getting excited and hoping that she was right and that there really was a secret passageway!

"But Heather…" Nate began, not wanting to upset his sister.

"The story says that the island belongs to Oak

Town… This island belongs to Elm Town. Well, it's a part of Elm Town," Nate told Heather.

"Yes, but Oak Town doesn't own any islands…" Heather informed.

"So maybe the people who discovered the passage-way said it was from an island belonging to Oak Town just to keep it a secret," Heather added.

"Hmm, so you're saying that the people who were in the Old Story of Oak Town Island wrote the story based on this island to keep it a secret and they said it was Oak Town Island just to make it sound like it was made up…" Nate understood, looking at Heather.
"Well, yes, but maybe!" Heather said.

"Because, there are no other islands, other than the ones near Elm Town's sea and they are not long lost so this is the only one that matches the island from the description in the story," Heather backed up.

"You know, Heather, I think you might be right!" exclaimed Nate!

"This is the only island that is long lost and matches the description from the story!" Nate exclaimed!

"The description said that it was an island far out off Elm Town's coast and had: a cove, a miniature beach, a harbour for boats, a cave and a cottage…" Heather reminded.

"That matches this island perfectly… Except, the cottage is half in ruins now," noticed Nate.

"Yeah," Heather said.

She looked at the beautiful island. It was tranquil and calm. The grass was a shade of fern green and the cottage was made from beige and cream coloured stones. There were wild birds and they were perched up high in the beautiful trees. On the island, the trees weren't just Oak trees, there were Elm trees, Willow trees and Maple trees and they all came together and made the island feel cosy – even though it was out to sea.

"Well, Nate, I don't know about you but I am very hungry!" Heather exclaimed, famished.

"I wonder what the time is," Nate pondered.

"It is very dark; we can barely see the island properly anymore," Nate commented.

"Yes, that's true!" Heather said, she too pondering what the time was.

"Let's go and find that cave and then we can get something to eat and find a place to sleep…"

"Okay."

Heather and Nate paced around the island, flashing their torch lights around; trying to find the cave. They wandered around the island; it was rather small (around half the size of a football pitch). After they explored the whole island, they didn't see the cave anywhere!

"Hmm that's peculiar!" Heather exclaimed.

"We searched the whole island yet we didn't manage to see the cave!" Nate finished.

"Yeah."

They paced around for a bit longer until Nate screamed before vanishing!...

Chapter 27

Where's Nate?

"Nate!" screamed Heather!

"Nate, where are you?!" she called, suddenly becoming very worried and concerned.

"I'm over here!" Nate said, his voice very muffled that you could barely hear what he said.

"Where?"

"Nate!"

"Where are you?" Heather cried, frantically looking around!

"I'm over here!" he replied.

"Nate! This isn't funny! Is this some sort of trick or practical joke!" Heather exclaimed, trying to follow the sound of Nate's voice.

"No!"

"Of course, this isn't a joke!" Nate exclaimed!

Then, he popped his head up from a hole in the ground and called to Heather:

"I found the cave!"

"Oh Nate!" laughed Heather.

Then, Heather ran towards the hole and looked down!

"The cave is underground!" she proclaimed, delighted that Nate had found it!

"Yeah!"

"Come down Heather!" Nate beckoned.

"How?" Heather pondered.

"Well, I just fell down into the cave but you can use this rope ladder," Nate said, gesturing at a sturdy rope ladder.

Heather smiled before making her way down.

Soon, she reached the bottom of the ladder and she jumped into the cave. Heather was expecting the floor to be stone but instead there was sand!

"Sand!"

"There's sand!" Heather exclaimed, running her fingers through the fine, white sand.

It was so nice to stand on and was very silky smooth.

"Yeah!"

"It's so nice!" Nate acknowledged!

"And look, Heather!" he said, before gesturing towards the crates of food and essentials pile up in the corner!

Heather's eyes widened at the sight of all that food.

"Wow!"

"Nate, these criminals really are being generous!" Heather said, looking at the food in glee.

"Yeah! They are much more generous than Don and his gang!" Heather said.

"I agree, but I mostly think that Jenny is the generous one!" Nate laughed.

"Yes."

"That's true!"

"When it's just Dan and Claude they are horrible to us!" Heather stated, grimly.

"Shall we have something to eat?"

"Yeah!"

"I'm starving!"

They said.

"What shall we eat?" pondered Heather, looking at the crates upon crates of food.

There were tins of vegetables, meat, fruit and many more. There were boxes of biscuits and chocolate; hanks of bread, cheese, butter, powdered custard and milk, packets of all sorts, a large jar of crunchy, sugar coated sweets and there were woven bags full of potatoes, carrots, mushrooms and many more vegetables that were waiting there to be boiled... There was a stove with pots and pans and also some sets of matches so that they could cook.

"Look, Heather, there is even a stove!" Nate exclaimed, pointing at the stove that was in the corner.

"Oh yes!" noticed Heather.

"Well, I doubt we will use it," Heather stated.

"What do you mean?"

"We will need it to cook vegetables on," Nate reminded, wondering what Heather had meant.

"Well, what I mean is that we will probably cook on an outdoor fire - as it might be dangerous to cook in here as we don't have much practice," Heather clarified.

"Oh yeah."

"Ok."

"Ok, let's just make some sandwiches," Heather said, before gathering some ingredients for sandwiches.

She gathered: four slices of bread (two each), some tomatoes, a couple of slices of cheese, some tinned meat, some vegetables and for afterwards some diced pineapple that was lightly covered in sugar and some chocolate biscuits; they also had some freshly squeezed orange juice... Heather and Nate quickly ate everything on their plates and their hungry stomachs were finally put to rest.

"Ahh!"

"That was a great meal!" Heather exclaimed.

"Yeah."

"Food always tastes so much better when it's eaten when you are hungry!" Nate declared.

"I agree!" Heather agreed, before standing up and brushing the sand off her skirt.

"Ahh."

"What are we going to do next?"

Nate yawned

"Well, Nate by the looks of it we need to go to sleep!" Heather declared, before she too yawned.

"Yes."

"That's a good idea – I'm tired!" Nate announced.

Then, both of them cleared their plates and then found some sleeping bags in amongst the crates of piled up items…

"I'm not sure about you, Nate, but I feel like sleeping outside in the open air!"

"Yeah! Come to think of it, so do it," Nate realized.

"This cave is rather stuffy!" he added.

Then, as Heather climbed back out of the cave something dropped out of her pocket and fell on the floor with a light thud.

What's that?" pondered Heather as she put her sleeping bag up on the ground and climbed back down the ladder to investigate.

Heather crouched down and picked up the thing that had fallen out of her pocket and she realized that it was the camera with all the evidence and photos from the criminals' secret room!

"Nate!"

"Here's the camera!"

"It was in my pocket the whole time!" Heather declared.

"Oh yes!"

"That's great!" Nate exclaimed.

On the ship the criminals took their bag so Heather and Nate had both assumed that they had taken their camera as well; but, Heather had taken it out and put it in her pocket last minute...

"Nate, you do realise that we still have a very vague idea of how the counterfeit money is even being spread across Oak Town," Heather reminded her younger brother.

"Yes."

"You are right, we know who are spreading them and where their base and everything else about the case but we don't know how!" Nate exclaimed, realizing how mysterious the situation actually was.

"Oh yeah!" Heather replied, pondering how mysterious it was.

"Well, maybe they break into shops in the middle of the night and steal all the money?" Nate suggested.

"I doubt it because that would be stealing and that's exactly what Barry, John and Don did last year…" Heather said.

"True," Nate agreed.

"It would be rather foolish of Dan to do exactly what his brother did last year," he added.

Heather nodded.

"Maybe they are finding a way to get to the source of the supply of real money and swap it with the fake…" Heather said.

"Maybe, but all the money printing factories are in Birch Town!" Nate replied, thinking hard.

"Wait!"

"Claude B!"

"Maybe he is doing most of this!" Nate blurted, rather suddenly.

"How?!"

"Go on Nate!" Heather encouraged.

"Well…" Nate began.

"Claude B was banned from Oak Town, right?"

"Yeah," Heather answered, wondering what Nate was on too.

"Well maybe he got a job in a factory and now he is using it to secretly swap the real precious money with the counterfeit notes!" Nate exclaimed.

"After all, all of Oak town's factories are in Birch Town. And Claude B wasn't banned from there!"

"Hmm," Heather pondered.

"And maybe he disguised himself so that no one would recognise him!" Nate interrupted, before Heather could say anything else!

"I'm not sure, Nate," Heather said, not wanting to upset Nate.

"It's a good theory but all the money from the factory would be packed and printed and there would be workers stationed at each process of the money making journey so if Claude B was doing something suspicious then some people would probably notice…" Heather reminded, thinking it would be almost impossible to find a way to swap the real money with the counterfeit money without someone noticing.

"That's true!" Nate acknowledged.

There was a long pause where they were both deep in thought but neither of them could think of a way the criminals could be doing this!

"Well," Nate said.

"I have a very strong feeling that your theory about this being the same island from the Old Story of Oak Town Island is correct. And, as it probably is – this means that the passageway under the ocean is here as well!" Nate added.

"So, let's start looking for the passageway right away!" Nate decided.

"In the story they said that the entrance to the

passageway was a large hole on the ground with a rusty metal ladder!" Nate recalled.

"Oh yes!" Heather remembered.

Nate yawned a huge yawn and almost immediately Heather did too!

"I think we should start looking first thing in the morning," Heather stated, tiredly.

"Yeah, good idea!" Nate agreed.

Then, Heather and Nate fell asleep almost instantly. They slept calmly on the soft grass and didn't even stir when an owl hooted from a tree that was right above them!...

Chapter 28

An Early Morning and a hunt

The next morning, Heather woke up as soon as the sunrise came and swiftly rolled her sleeping bag away and went down into the cave to make breakfast. Heather made some toast (which was just bread smothered with jam and butter as they had no toaster) and she poured some fresh orange juice out of a glass bottle. Heather carried the food up onto the island and then woke Nate up.

"Nate!"

"Nate!"

"Wake up!" she awakened.

Nate yawned and rubbed his eyes to wake himself up and then they both chatted for a bit before having some breakfast.

"Alright," Heather began.

"So today we will go around the island to try and find the entrance to the secret passageway under the ocean," Heather planned.

"Ok," Nate said.

"Wait."

"Heather, if there was a massive passageway entrance, wouldn't the criminals have already noticed it when they came here and covered it up or filled it?" Nate realized.

"Oh," Heather began.

"I hadn't thought of that!" she concluded.

"Yeah," Nate responded.

"Well, there is no harm in looking anyway!" Nate said.

"We have nothing else to do anyway," he stated.

"Yes."

"Ok."

"Let's start looking then," Heather declared.

"How about you search from that side of the island and I start searching from that side... Then, we will cover more ground in less time," Heather planned, strategically, pointing to either side of the island.

"Ok, sounds like a plan!" Nate grinned, before running off to the other end of the island and began hunting for clues to the entrance to the passage under the ocean...

Heather dashed over to her side of the island and then she too started to search. Neither Heather nor Nate knew what to look for but they just assumed that if they found the entrance, they would know...

After an hour or so, Heather and Nate had both met back in the middle of the island and had found nothing.

"I didn't find anything," Nate sighed.

"Me neither," Heather frowned.

"Hmm, maybe we are stranded on this island after all," Heather said, looking down to the ground in dismay.

Nate sighed miserably.

"Wait!"

"Oh my goodness!" Heather exclaimed.

"Look at this!" she said before crouching down and pointing to a thin bit of worn out rope!

Nate frowned, puzzled.

Heather was pulling at the rope and to her pleasure it was getting longer and was becoming thicker and stronger!

Soon, it became too hard to pull by herself so Nate helped her and they both pulled at the rope together! Heather and Nate were picking up pace and now they had a flow going to the rope pulling...

After a while, the rope came to an abrupt stop and Heather and Nate realized that the rope was coming from a patch of artificial grass. They pulled away a neatly cut patch of artificial grass and underneath that there was a metal square that was about the size of an average, circular dining table! Heather and Nate ran over to where the patch of grass had formerly been and there was a large hole with a rusty, decaying metal ladder...

Heather and Nate's eyes widened and glistened with happiness, excitement and adventure.

"We found it!" they exclaimed in unison!

Chapter 29

Escape under the ocean

"Come on!"

"Let's go!" Nate exclaimed, jumping up and down in delight.

"Wait," Heather commanded, before Nate was about to jump into the hole that opened up into the passageway.

"We need to get some supplies," Heather remarked.

"What do you mean?" Nate asked, mightily confused.

"What I mean is that if this is the passageway that will take us under the ocean back to Oak Town then we need to pack some food and torches and stuff, as the passageway will be very long…" Heather clarified.

"Oh ok."

"Yeah, that's true."

"In that case we will need a lot of stuff like lunch and maybe some sleeping bags as well in case we end up needing to spend the night in the passageway," Nate suggested.

"Oh yeah."

"Well, in that case let's not waste another moment and get back to the cave to start packing," Nate declared, before running towards the cave.

Heather ran after her brother and then they both jumped down into the dark, musty, resourceful cave.

"Ok, let's take some food," Heather said, before grabbing some biscuits and fruit and placing them in a potato sack.

Heather packed loads of different food into the bag while Nate filled another potato sack to the brim with essentials like blankets, sleeping bags, torches, chalk so they could mark their route in case they needed to make an emergency trip back or if they got lost! Soon, Heather and Nate had packed everything they needed and not to forget, the camera, so that they could show the police the images for proof!

"I think we are ready to go now, Nate," Heather announced, taking a final look around to see if there was anything else that they would need.

"Yeah."

"I think we are ready to go!" Nate announced, excitedly.

Then, they both excitedly scampered out of the cave and ran back to the entrance to the passageway...

"Wait!"

"I'll be right back!" Nate vocalized dramatically.

"Ok," shrugged Heather, slightly puzzled.

A couple of minutes later, Nate was back and he was holding two shovels while still clutching the potato sack that was full of their essential supplies…

"Oh yes!"

"Shovels! Great idea, Nate!" Heather congratulated.

"It's in case the tunnel has been blocked by rocks every now and again. Then with the shovels we can dig our way through!" Nate laughed.

Heather grinned.

"Come on then, let's go!" she declared, leading the way into the hole.

Heather jumped into the hole and then beckoned Nate to throw the supplies in for her to catch.

Heather caught the supplies and then Nate too jumped in!

"When they were down in the hole there was a small hole that they crawled through into and instantly it opened up into a slightly bigger, wider and taller tunnel. Heather and Nate crawled steadily but slowly through the passageway. It was wide enough for them to crawl – not walk – and they had to be in single file with the potato sacks of supplies strapped to their backs and the shovels being pushed in front of them.

"This is really tight!" Nate muttered, feeling the desperate urge to stretch his legs.

"Yeah, let's just hope soon the passage extends and gets larger," Heather replied, trying to sound positive.

"I hope so," Nate hoped.

Heather and Nate crawled for around another ten minutes before the passage finally expanded and slowly but surely was become larger... At first, the ceiling became higher and then the walls expanded.

"Nate! The passageway is becoming larger!" Heather enunciated, with glee.

"Yes!" Nate said in triumph, then he slowly stood up and walked in a half crouched and as the passage became larger, he soon was able to walk normally!

"Ahh!"

"It feels great to stand up!" he announced.

"My knees are so sore with all the crawling!" Heather grumbled, rubbing her sore knees!

"Yeah, same here!" Nate related.

"Should we have something to eat?" Nate wondered, his eyes darting to the potato sack filled with food!

"Yes."

"That's a good idea as we are in a very good spot in the passageway," Heather examined.

"Yeah," Nate agreed.

By now the passage became so large that it was about the size of a small room! Heather and Nate noticed that the passageway wasn't going to get any larger for a while so they decided it would be best if they made a quick stop for a meal...

Heather and Nate both sat down on the cold, cobbled floor. They took some things out of the potato sack, like: some tinned fruit, a tin opener, some biscuits, a helping of cheese and crackers and a tiny bit of water each (they were rationing the water as they didn't know when they would be able to refill their flask)... They both hungrily gobbled up all the food and then sat down for a bit before setting off once more...

Chapter 30

The end of the passageway
– and a dead end

Heather and Nate continued to steadily crawl through the passageway and they made the right call to stop at where they stopped as the passageway only got smaller! They were at a part where the ceiling got precariously low!

"Should we try and dig our way through, a bit?" Nate suggested, as they squeezed through the passage.

"I wish we could but we are under the ocean so it could be risky if we try and dig…" Heather reminded, wisely.

"Oh yeah, that's true!" Nate shrieked, only just remembering that they were underwater.

Heather giggled.

"Yeah, well the last thing we want is to crack the walls or ceiling because that will flood the tunnel!" Heather added.

Nate shivered, trying not to imagine the passage flooding.

Heather noticed that Nate looked startled so she gave him a comforting pat on the back.

Nate smiled and then they carried on crawling.

After a while, Heather and Nate came to an abrupt halt as the passageway ended and it was perfectly closed off by a cobbled wall.

"The passageway has just ended!" Nate announced, taken aback.

"It looks like someone has built a wall here to block it off!" Heather examined, running her fingers across the wall.

"Yes."

"Although, the wall looks old!" Nate exclaimed.

"It doesn't look like it has been put here in the last one hundred years!" He commented.

"That's true."

"By the looks of it the wall has been here as long as the passage has," Heather agreed, examining.

"Yeah, that's true."

"But then, how did the explorer go through the passageway and then come out of it back on Oak Town?" Nate pondered, trying to piece all the pieces of the puzzle together.

"Maybe, he made people block the passageway after his adventure," Heather sighed.

"Maybe," Nate replied, crestfallen.

"I guess we will have to go back now!" Nate announced.

"I'm afraid so!" Heather replied.

"Although," Nate began.

"I don't particularly want to go back to the island," he continued.

"Why?" Heather asked.

"Is it because, we will have to crawl another five miles or so?" Heather asked, not really making the journey back feel very positive.

"Well, no. It's because…"

"We are in Oak Town!" Nate reminded.

Heather was confused, she thought for a moment.

"Oh my!"

"Yes!"

"Yes, we are!" she realized.

"We are so close but we can't get out of this passageway."

Heather rested her head against the cobbled wall and sighed. Nate did the same thing but he rested his head against a stone that bulged out of the wall so he cried:

"Ouch!"

"That hurt!" he cried, rubbing his head.

"What?!" asked Heather who had been staring at the cobbled wall that was parallel to the one she had her head against!

"I banged my head against this annoying rock that is sticking out of the wall in the most ambiguous manner!" Nate told his sister.

"Oh," Heather said.

"Are you ok?"

"Yeah," he replied.

"This stone is weird," Nate observed.

"How?" Heather pondered, looking at the stone.

"It looks newer than the rest and it sticks out," Nate clarified.

"Oh yeah."

Nate pushed the stone, trying to get it to fit back in it's place in the wall and then the most perplexing rumble came from nowhere...

Chapter 31

It all happens fast

Heather and Nate held on to each other in a state of pure fright.

"What's that noise?!" Nate wailed.

"No idea!" Heather replied, feeling very shocked.

The noise rumbled on for another couple of minutes or so and Heather and Nate had no idea what to do so they just listened and waited... Dramatically, the monotonous rumble came to an abrupt halt and the wall that was blocking the passageway had smoothly slid away. To reveal a ladder that went straight up...

Heather and Nate grinned in awe.

"Let's go!" Heather exclaimed, leading the way up the ladder.

Heather and Nate climbed up the ladder, soon feeling the cool breeze hitting their face. After, they heard the wall sliding back and the passage closing once more. After they both got to the top of the ladder it opened up into a cave!

"Nate! We are in a cave!" Heather announced.

Nate came climbed into the cave from the ladder and then they both looked around.

"Where are we?" pondered Nate.

"Let's get out of this cave and then it might be easier to see where we are…" Heather pointed out.

"We were crawling through the passageway for around eight hours now so it would be the evening and because we were crawling for so long, we are probably up back in the North of Oak Town…" Heather told, strategically.

"Oh yes."

"That's true."

"Well, what are we waiting for!"

"Let's go!" Nate jumped, leading the way out of the cave.

Heather followed her brother and then they realized where they were…

"Oh my!" Heather gasped.

"We are in the woods that is very near the abandoned house!" she exclaimed.

"The last thing we want now is for the criminals to spot us and take us somewhere to be held captive!" Nate shivered.

"Oh yes," Heather replied.

"That would be utterly terrible!" she cried.

There was a pause.

"Wait."

"Where are we planning on going?" Nate asked.

"Well, we need to go to the police department and tell them about our adventure and discovery; and then after that we will go with them to the factory - to find out how the criminals swapped the counterfeit money with the real money - and then to the abandoned house to see the base where the criminals are making the counterfeit money; and then to the port of Elm Town to catch the criminals and the police will arrest them..." Heather planned.

"Yes, that's a good idea!" Nate approved.

"So, come on then. Let's go!" Nate said, before starting to run to the police department.

"Wait! Nate! Stop running!"

Nate ran back to his sister and then shrugged and said:

"We need to get to the police department as soon as possible!"

"I know!"

"But we need to be careful..."

"How about we split up?" she suggested.

"What do you mean?" Nate pondered.

"I mean, how about you go to the police department first and ten minutes later I go..." she stated.

"Oh yeah! So, either way if one of us gets caught then the other one of us can tell the police about our adventure and stop the criminals; then also send a search party to find where the other one of us went!" Nate finished.

"Precisely!" Heather agreed.

"So, can I go first?" Nate wondered.

"Yeah, okay," Heather appointed.

"And, you can take the camera," she said, handing him the camera.

"You go first and around ten minutes later I will go," she informed.

"Ok."

Then, Nate sped off.

Heather went into the cave and then waited... Heather sat down on a rock and patiently waited what she thought was around ten minutes before she too raced to the police department. Heather left her bag in the cave as it was just full of the things that they needed in the underwater passageway...!

After around ten minutes of full paced sprinting and then five minutes of jogging; Heather reached the police department and quickly stumbled inside.

Heather was greeted.

"Hello Heather! Nate has started telling us a bit about your adventure... Please come with me to a side room where all the officers are waiting..." PC Jones ushered.

Heather went into the room where Nate was already seated with a hot water bottle and then she was handed one as well. After that, PC Jones came back and said that they had closed the police department and other officers were on their way as all the town's police force needed to hear Heather and Nate's story... After that, Chief Andrew came in with another troop of officers and then they knew that they were ready to begin...

Chapter 32

The story

"Nate!"

"Heather!" greeted the Chief before shaking their hands!

"I came as soon as I found out that you have solved the case and I have called your Parents and Grandparents so they should be here soon!" He informed, warmly.

Then, Chief Andrew sat down and Heather and Nate began telling their story...

How they were staying with their Grandparents over the holidays and how when they went to the station, they saw a porter that they thought they recognized...

How when they then saw in the newspaper that there was counterfeit money being spread through Oak Town.

How from their grandparents' attic they saw an abandoned house and Heather thought she saw a light.

Then, when they went to the post office, they saw the porter as a newspaper man!

How they decided to follow the mysterious man to see where he goes and how they waited by the house of the final person on the newspaper delivery list then followed the man to see where he goes next.

How he went to the abandoned house and then he gave a letter to an artist.

How they talked to the artist and how she told them never to go near the house and how Nate thought that he had seen Don in the house.

After that, they went to the police department and asked if Don was still there and he was!

How after, they went on a camping trip to go and investigate the house and how they were trapped in the house. How they went around the house to go and investigate and see if they could find where the secret base was in the house.

They found the identity cards of the criminals and found out the person who looked like Don was his brother – Dan; the artist was called Jenny – even though they already knew that; and that the mysterious man was actually Claude Bernard – one of Oak Town's fired police officers! (When Heather and Nate said this the police officers gasped and sat up straight!).

How, they explored the house and found the counterfeit money up on the top floor and how they had a sample of it. (Nate handed the officers a note of counterfeit money from his pocket).

Then, how they went downstairs to the library and

when Heather took a book from the shelves and there was a loud rumble and then a wall slid away to reveal a set of stairs.

Then, how they both went down and then they came to the place where the criminals were manufacturing the counterfeit money. (Nate showed the police the pictures they had taken)...

After that how they were going to escape from the house but the criminals captured them and then took them all the way to the port of Elm Town and then boarded them onto a ship.

How they had been taken across the ocean on the ship and taken to an island. How they were prisoner on the island but then realized that the island they were on was the island from a story in the book of Stories of Oak Town.

How that in the story an explorer discovered a way to go from the island all the way to Oak Town - via a passage under the ocean!

And, how they discovered the passage and crawled all the way through it back to Oak Town.

Penultimately how you had to press a stone to get out of the passage and into the cave that it ended in.

Finally, how Heather and Nate made their separate journeys to the police department to ensure that if one of them was caught the other could get the police's help...

After the story was over the officers looked at each other in awe.

"Wow!"

"I can't believe you two did all that," Chief Andrew announced in awe.

"Yes!"

"That was superb!" congratulated the officers.

"Brilliant!"

"Amazing!"

"The town is safe because of you!"

Cheers of congratulation erupted from all over the meeting room and Heather and Nate beamed.

"I will arrange for some sort of reward for you two but first we need to stop those criminals!" Chief Andrew bellowed.

"Heather and Nate, do you have any idea how the criminals are spreading the counterfeit money, right?"

"Well, we assumed that the money must somehow be getting swapped at the money printing factory in Birch Town – we are just unsure how it is happening with all the workers there..." Heather informed, swiftly.

"Alright, thank you! Well, I will arrange for a troop of officers to go to the factory and find out..." Chief Andrew planned.

"And you said that the criminals are planning to leave Oak Town from the port of Elm Town in the middle of the month, right?"

"The criminals said that they would leave mid month," Nate responded.

"Ok."

"So, they would still be in the abandoned house now," Chief Andrew said to himself.

"So, first, around ten officers and I, will go to the money printing factory in Birch Town to investigate how the criminals are swapping the real money for the counterfeit money, while another ten officers go to the abandoned house and catch the criminals. Then, five officers will go to the port of Elm Town so that if the criminals try to make a run for it and try to flee across the ocean.

"Do they have a boat in the harbour?" Chief Andrew asked.

"Yes."

"They have a large ship," Nate responded.

"Ok."

"I give the officers who will be stationed at the port: the authority to search their ship," appointed Chief Andrew.

"Now, officers: Jones, Brown, David, Timothy, Lee, Williams, Johnson, Karl, Miller and Harris; I want you officers to come with me to the factory."

"Officers: Clark, Walker, Young, Allen, Scott, Baker, Roberts, Campbell, Hall and King; I want you officers to go to the abandoned house."

"And finally, officers: Anderson, Thomas, Martin, Bell and Gordon; I want you to go to the Port of Elm Town and explore the ship whilst being on guard," Chief Andrew commanded.

"If something happens: like, you arrest the criminals I would like you to alert me immediately!" he conducted.

All the officers nodded in unison.

"Now, Heather and Nate, I would like one of you to go to the abandoned house and I want one of you to come with me to the factory..." The Chief said to them.

"It's up to you who goes where," he added.

"I'll go to the factory," Nate said, he was very eager to find out how the criminals managed to spread the counterfeit money without all the other workers in the factory knowing!

"In that case I will go to the abandoned house!" Heather said, although she also wanted to go to the factory, she didn't make a fuss!

"Alright then."

"In that case let's not waste another moment!" Chief Andrew said to the officers.

"Oh, and by the way, Heather and Nate..." he

began.

"Your Parents and Grandparents will be here at nine o'clock at night. By then our investigations will be over and the criminals will be captured..." he finished.

"Chief Andrew, there must be some mistake. Our Parents are away," Heather reminded.

"Oh yes," Nate realized.

"Coincidentally their business trip has ended short!" clapped the Chief.

Heather and Nate grinned.

After that, the troops set off in their separate ways...

Chapter 33

The Factory

Nate, a troop of officers and Chief Andrew were all in police cars and were on their way to the money printing factory in Birch Town. They zoomed through Oak Town, then through Maple Town and then they came to Birch Town... Nate looked around eagerly. Birch Town was very different to Oak Town. It was very industrial and had loads of factories and large buildings – yet, it still had loads of Birch trees! After that, they came to the money printing factory and the police officers (followed by Nate) stormed inside.

To their utmost shock, there by one of the machines was Claude B! There was no one else there and he hadn't seen the troop of officers or Nate enter... Chief Andrew gestured for the officers to surround Claude from a distance in case he tries to make a run for it... Then, Claude turned around and gasped.

"H – h – how did you get here?!" he stammered, looking around for a way to escape.

"You will be the one answering questions," smirked PC Lee.

"How did you escape?!" roared Claude pointing an accusing finger at Nate.

Nate was startled and stepped back. Chief Andrew put a protecting hand over Nate.

"I knew you were a bad officer but I never knew you would become a criminal!" Chief Andrew muttered to Claude.

Claude gulped. Seeing all his old officers and his old boss like this was very traumatizing!

"Claude," began Chief Andrew…

"How have you been spreading the counterfeit money?" asked the chief.

"I'm not telling you!" howled Claude, stubbornly.

"I never will," he added.

"Oh yes you will," snarled Chief Andrew.

"If you tell us now and return the real money to Oak Town then we will let you go with no punishment," Chief Andrew lied, trying to coax the answers out of Claude.

"My lips are sealed," Claude screamed.

"Well, then, we will take you in for interrogation…" Chief Andrew shrugged.

Claude B gulped. As his time as an officer, he had once conducted an interrogation and it was a very intimidating experience!

Then, swiftly, the officers hand cuffed Claude B and he was taken to one of the police cars to sit quietly with PC Lee!

"Alright, now that he's out off the way let's get down to business."

"We need to find out why all the factory workers aren't here."

"And we need to shut these machines down because all the money that is going through them and being boxed up and to be taken to the near by banks is counterfeit," he added.

"Ok."

"Sure."

"Yes," responded the officers.

"Look, up there! There is an emergency switch to switch all the machines off!" Nate remarked, pointing at the switch that was high up on the wall.

"Oh yeah."

"Great spotting, Nate!" congratulated Chief Andrew.

Nate beamed.

Quickly and efficiently, PC Brown located a ladder and with the help of some other officers they managed to reach the switch and push it. After doing so, all the machines turned off and came to a sudden halt.

Now that the factory was all quiet, the officers began to hear another rather alarming noise... It was the sound of people banging on glass. It was coming from somewhere in the factory...

"Officers, follow that sound!" commanded Chief Andrew.

Nate followed them all.

"It's coming from upstairs!" PC Brown told them all, listening intently.

All officers tiptoed upstairs, following the sound. Soon, they got to the second floor of the factory and there was a meeting room with loads of factory workers inside – by the looks of it they were trapped! The officers (lead by chief Andrew) darted to the room and swiftly unlocked the door that was craftily locked from the outside!

"Thank you!"

"Thanks!"

"You saved us!"

"Thank you so much!" came cries of thank from the factory workers who were trapped inside the meeting room.

"Why were you trapped in there?" Chief Andrew asked, pointing at the room.

"These people - I think they were called Dan and Claude locked us up in here when we were having a meeting!" informed a flustered woman.

"Yes, and Claude was actually on a job trial here!" chirped a young man.

Chief Andrew pulled a pocketbook from his pocket

and took some notes, before nodding for the man to continue.

"We have been in the meeting room for six days now and we have been living off food from our four vending machines and food from the box of food that were thankfully put here last minute!" added the man.

"So, Claude B has locked you guys up in there and he has been taking over the factory?" asked Chief Andrew, wanting to clarify that.

"Yes."

"And he sent letters to all our families saying that we will be staying at the factory overnight for a week maybe longer. And, took away our phones. So, that our families aren't suspicious," piped a tall man with a long beard.

"Oh my!" gasped Chief Andrew.

"That Claude keeps taking it too far!" he uttered, shaking his head in dismay.

"I agree," agreed PC Jones.

And all the other officers nodded. Then, Chief Andrew turned to Nate.

"You said he was working with Dan – Don's brother, right?"

"Yes," Nate responded.

"Ok, thank you," thanked the Chief.

"And, is Dan at the abandoned house," he understood.

That reminds me, I must call the officers at the abandoned house to tell them that we have captured Claude.

Then, Chief Andrew took his phone out of his pocket made a phone call.

"Hello!"

Pause

"Oh yes!"

Pause

"Yes."

Pause

"I called to say that we have got Claude Bernard and he is in the car with PC Lee…"

Pause

"Ok."

Pause

"Cool."

Pause

"We also worked out how the criminals were managing to spread the counterfeit money."

Pause

"They had trapped all the factory workers and they were running the factory themselves!"

Pause

"Yes."

Pause

"I will tell you and all the other officers the full case later."

Pause

"Yes."

Pause

"See you back in the police department soon!"

Pause

"Bye for now!"

"That was PC Walker on the phone," informed Chief Andrew.

"They are just about to go and capture Dan and Jenny! I hope they manage it successfully!"

"Thanks to Heather and Nate we have very almost solved the case and now Oak Town can be returned to it's former glory!" proclaimed the Chief clapping with delight.

The officers nodded in approval. Then, they set off. They had all exited the factory and they had boarded the police cars to return to the police department.

Chapter 34

At the abandoned house

Back at the abandoned house Heather was with a troop of officers and they had just managed to arrest Dan and Jenny.

Heather and the officers had abruptly burst into the abandoned house and Heather had told the police officers where all the entrances and the exits to the house were and one officer was stationed at each, so the criminals wouldn't be able to make a run for it!

The officers entered the house and thoroughly searched it before realizing the criminals were no where to be seen. So, Heather led them to the opening of the passageway to the secret room and they stealthily tiptoed through it until they reached the secret base where the counterfeit money was being printed. Heather and the police officers could here the whir of machines and they heard a conversation between Dan and Jenny going on in the secret room – although, their conversation was not audible... After that, the police officers and Heather burst into the secret room and Dan and Jenny were in the middle of the room and were scared out of their skin and they jumped up in fright.

"Stop in the name of the law!" exclaimed Jenny.

Heather giggled. The police officers were slightly confused but swiftly closed in on Jenny and Dan.

"W – w – why are you h – here?" mumbled Dan.

"You're busted Dan!" smirked PC Baker.

"We know everything you have done!" added PC Walker.

And all the other officers nodded in approval.

Dan tried to make a run for it by running to the door that exited the secret room but police officers were already stationed there so as Dan ran out, they captured him and put a slick pair of silver hand cuffs on him and escorted him to the car… After that, Jenny was also arrested – although, she shouted many strange things in her defence, like:

"I'm innocent!"

"I was bribed!"

"They said I could have a polar bear if I did the job!"

"I can't go to jail as I am allergic to bricks!"

"Can you make me prisoner in my house instead?"

The police officers took no nonsense and just tried not to laugh at Jenny's eccentric behaviour! After the criminals were handcuffed and loaded into the police cars, they were driven away to the police department for further interrogation…

"What are you going to do now?" asked Heather.

"What do you mean?" asked PC Allen.

"Like, what are you going to do to the abandoned house? Are you going to dismantle the machines and get all the counterfeit money from the attic?" clarified Heather.

"Well, throughout the next few days we will continue investigating the house and then we will also investigate the factory; return money to people who have received counterfeit money and then we will be done with the case!" responded PC Allen.

"Oh ok," Heather replied.

"I wonder how they are doing at the factory?" she asked herself.

"Oh my! That reminds me! I must make a call to tell Chief Andrew that we captured Jenny and Dan!" PC Walker replied, before getting out his special police officers' phone and making a call.

"Hello, Chief!"

Pause

"Yes!"

Pause

"We have captured Jenny and Dan!"

Pause

"And we are on our way back to the police department!"

Pause

"Ok."

Pause

"Sure."

Pause

"I'll see you soon!"

Pause

"Bye Chief Andrew."

Pause

"Bye bye!"

Then, the officer put his phone back in his pocket and turned around to the troop of officers in the car.

The police car was very large, and although it was labelled a car, it was more like a minibus!

"Well, thanks to Heather and Nate, Oak Town is safe once more!" exclaimed PC Walker, and a cheer broke out; however, to everyone's surprise, Jenny joined in with the cheering!

Dan growled. He hated to have known that the police officers and Heather and Nate had gotten the better off him, Claude and Jenny.

"How did you silly children get off the island?" asked Dan, pointing an accusing finger at Heather.

"Well, um, you see there is a secret pass - !" Heather began before she was interrupted by PC Roberts.

"That's none of your business, Dan!" cried PC Roberts, shaking his head.

"What do you mean done of you biscuits?!" asked Jenny!

"I wasn't informed of any biscuits!"

"I love biscuits!" she howled.

"I want biscuits!" she wailed.

Heather laughed. Dan shook his head. And, the police officers tried not to laugh as it would seem unprofessional!

Then, the police minibus pulled up into the police department... Oak Town had three police departments, one was in the South and the other in the North; and they had a smaller one with a couple of officers in the East...

Heather and the officers got out of the police minibus and then PC King and PC Baker escorted Dan and Jenny out of the minibus. Dan was trying to run but it was hard when he was handcuffed. Jenny, on the other hand, didn't try and escape in the slightest! Instead, she said to the officers:

"Hurry up and take me inside for interrogation! It's allergy season!"

Swiftly, the police officers had all gone back into the police department and they had taken Dan and Jenny inside and sat them down in an interrogation room. But Dan was still trying to run away so PC Clark had to handcuff him to a chair so that all that he could do was sit on the chair!

"We will come back later to interrogate you two!" PC Clark informed.

"Okay!" Jenny exclaimed, cheerily.

Dan growled aggressively.

Then, PC Clark exited the room and locked the door behind him...

Chapter 35

The reunion

Heather and Nate's Parents and Grandparents were on their way to the police department and Nate and the officers who were at the factory had just pulled up in the police department...

"Let me go!"

"Leave me alone!"

"You guys were my old colleagues!" wailed Claude B.

"Well, now we most certainly are not!" Chief Andrew bellowed.

Claude B scowled.

And the officers rolled their eyes at him and then they swiftly shooed Claude into the police department and then he was taken into the room where Dan and Jenny were already waiting...

Also, Heather was reunited with Nate!

"Nate!" Heather exclaimed as she ran towards her brother.

"Heather!" Nate exclaimed in response!

Heather and Nate greeted one another as they reunited. They both quickly chattered and exchanged news about what happened and what was going on in the factory and abandoned house! Nate told his sister how the criminals had imprisoned the factory workers in the meeting room; took over the factory and then swapped all the real money for counterfeit money. Then, Heather told Nate the story of how the police captured Jenny and Dan from the secret room in the abandoned house! While Heather and Nate were busy nattering, they didn't realize that their Parents and Grandparents had entered the police department!

"Heather!"

"Nate!" exclaimed their Parents before striding towards them!

"Mum!"

"Dad!" Heather and Nate shouted, happily.

And, their Grandparents followed swiftly. After that, the reunited family were together again and they exchanged news...

"We are so happy you are safe!" announced Mum.

"I can't believe you had another adventure!"

"You two saved Oak Town again!"

"Well done Heather and Nate!"

Heather, Nate, their Parents and their Grandparents then caught up with each other and exchanged news. Then, Heather and Nate told them the story of their adventure... And how after, with the help of the police department, they captured the criminals and solved the mystery of how the counterfeit money were being spread...

"Wow!"

"That's an amazing story!"

"That must have been a hair raising adventure to be a part of!"

For a while, the family continued to talk and ask questions and Heather and Nate continued to fill them in; and, tell them all the details of their adventure. In addition, Heather and Nate told them everything that Jenny had said and misunderstood!

After around half an hour, Chief Andrew came over to the family and told them that they had finished interrogating Dan, Claude and Jenny and that the officers had made them tell them everything about what they were doing... So, now the criminals were going to go to jail!

Heather and Nate cheered! Their adventure was worth it! They saved their town – again!

"So, Heather and Nate, we are eternally grateful to what you have done for the town and so, tomorrow we have a surprise for you," Chief Andrew explained, smiling broadly.

Heather and Nate beamed and wondered what the surprise could be. After that, Heather, Nate and their Parents and Grandparents left the police department and made their way to their Grandparents' house so that they could spend the night there before going to back to their home in the Southeast and then they would have their surprise!

Chapter 36

Back home – and the surprise

The following morning, after breakfast, Heather and Nate went to the station with all their luggage that they had taken to their Grandparents' house and they were waiting for the next train... Because Oak Town was a small town, there were only two trains and when one was going up through Oak Town, the other would be going down, meaning there would usually be around a half an hour wait until the next train would come to the station... So, to keep them going, Heather and Nate bought a drink and some biscuits from the station café! Soon after, the train arrived and the family boarded it happily. They sped through Oak Town and Heather and Nate reflected on their adventure... They couldn't believe that just not too long ago they were going to their Grandparents' house on this very train and back then Nate was just hoping for an adventure! Heather and Nate talked about this and then about their entire adventure all over again until they pulled up in Southern Oak Town Station.

"Come on then, let's go home!" announced Mum before leading the way out of the train.

Heather and Nate looked around and smiled. They were home. Back to the emerald green, dew coated grass, fewer Oak trees and patches of stunningly colourful flowers. The family all walked back to their house from the station. It was a twenty minute walk back to their house and Nate was whining!

"Why can't we get the taxi?!" he moaned!

"Because, the taxi's will take twenty minutes to get here!" Dad replied.

"How do you know?" Nate wailed.

"Because, your Mum and I checked the taxi availability at the station," Dad answered.

"Oh," sighed Nate, before grumbling, slouching and then walking again – dragging his luggage behind him!

After around another fifteen minutes of walking, the family reached their house and to Heather and Nate's surprise there were two cardboard packages on the doorstep!

"What are these?" Nate asked, inquisitively.

"Mum and Dad, what are these packages?" Heather pondered, eyeing the packages.

"Well, let's put our luggage inside and then we can come back and take them in to open," Mum planned, as she put the house key into the lock and twisted to unlock the front door.

Heather and Nate stepped inside then put their bags down and dashed back outside so that they could help their Parents with the rest of the luggage and then to bring in the parcels!

"Thank you, you two!" thanked Dad.

"It's ok."

"No problem," Heather and Nate replied before Dad carried the two parcels into the living room.

Heather and Nate tore the cardboard packaging off the boxes to reveal clothes! But, not just any old clothes... Heather had an emerald, green dress that glistened and sparkled in the light and it had a silver cardigan and a silver hair band with shiny velvet and jewels on it! Nate had a black suit with a crisp white shirt and black tie; there were also a pair of black trousers...

Heather and Nate gasped at the dress and suit! These were the most extravagant clothes they had ever been given!

"Woah!" gaped Heather, gasping at her dress in awe.

"Wow!" gasped Nate.

"I will look like a spy in this suit!" he exclaimed.

Everyone laughed!

"What are these fancy new clothes for anyway?" Heather asked.

Nate also eagerly listened for the answer.

"Well," began Mum.

"This afternoon there will be a tea party in our garden and you two will be receiving a special award…" Dad finished, smiling at them.

Heather and Nate looked at each other and there were eyes were filled with excitement!

"What award is it?" asked Nate.

"We ourselves don't know yet!" admitted Mum.

"Okay," Nate replied.

"And, as it will be set up in our garden, it is going to be a surprise for you so we would like you both to go into the study as it only has one window that overlooks the front of the house so you won't be able to see how the preparations in the garden are going…" Dad stated.

"Ok," Heather and Nate replied in unison.

Then, there was a knock on the door… The first things for the garden party had arrived!

Chapter 37

The Garden Party and ceremony

For the rest of the day Heather and Nate were in the study working on a massive puzzle! From the study they had been constantly hearing the ring of the doorbell or knocks on the door! And Heather and Nate could hear the voices of people coming through the door and dropping stuff off... From what they could hear they also heard loads of people in the garden building things and chatting loudly.

"I wonder what is going on in the garden," Nate wondered.

"Yeah."

"I can't wait for the party later!" Heather exclaimed, ecstatic!

"Me neither!" Nate pronounced, overjoyed.

And so, Heather and Nate waited and waited and waited some more and even finished the puzzle before Mum and Dad had come into the study.

"All the guests are already here and waiting in the garden..." Mum began.

"Wow!" Dad interrupted.

"I can't believe you both finished that puzzle!" Dad exclaimed, surprised.

Mum smiled.

"It's time for you both to change into your new clothes," Mum explained.

Then, they were handed their new clothes and Nate went to change in the bathroom while Heather stayed in the study.

Soon, they were both ready and changed and they were finally allowed out into the garden. Heather and Nate both looked very smart in their new clothes! Mum quickly took some pictures of them both in front of the door and then they had to close their eyes and Mum and Dad led them both out into the garden.

They stepped out into the garden and they opened their eyes and instantly they lit up!

There was a very long table that ran all the way down their massive garden and it was piled high with food, drinks, desserts and anything you could think of! There were sandwiches of all sorts and even sandwiches that Heather and Nate hadn't heard of! There was a massive bowl with a fruit salad and smaller dishes that were piled high with fresh cream. Crackers, pretzels and savoury biscuits were stacked and piled high and were surrounded by bowls of dipping sauce, hummus, butter and avocado guacamole. There were wraps that were filled with vegetables, egg and other fillings and were cut in half with a thin wooden stick through them – holding the wrap together. There were cupcakes with strawberry, chocolate, vanilla and pistachio icing. There were cubes of fruit that were diced in sugar. Gingerbread was snapped into small square like shapes and large mugs of lemonade, orange juice, apple juice, water, icy cold water and mugs of cold tea. At the end of the table there was a towering vanilla cake with four tiers and was beautifully decorated; it had fondant icing Oak trees with adorable little animals and butterflies! And all sorts of other food... On the grass there were loads of picnic blankets with Heather and Nate's: friends, family, cousins, police officers and other friendly townsfolk that Heather and Nate's Parents were friends with. Heather and Nate's tree house had brilliant bunting on it and there was bunting all around the garden! At the end of the garden there was a miniature stage! There were also colourful lights all around the garden – to switch on in case it got dark.

Heather and Nate gasped at the way the garden was decorated and then a cheer erupted around the garden.

"Well done!"

"Bravo."

"Three cheers!"

And many more shouts of congratulation were made. After that, the Mayor spoke through the microphone and said:

"Heather and Nate, we would like to come together

as a community to congratulate you for saving the town once again! Please join me on stage to be presented with your reward..."

Heather and Nate proudly walked up onto the stage and then the Mayor stood in the centre of the stage and Heather and Nate stood beside him. Then, the Mayor gave a speech.

"Heather and Nate, you two have saved Oak Town once again. Last time from thieves and this time from criminals who were manufacturing counterfeit money! And that itself is a rather queer crime – if I do say so myself!" laughed the Mayor, a laugh going around the garden.

After that, the Mayor told the crowd the story of Heather and Nate's adventure and Heather and Nate helped him by adding parts in and making parts more detailed!

Then, after they had finished, the Mayor said: "As we all know, last year when you saved the town for the first time, you were both given the Oak Town Award of Gratitude and that is an award for townsfolk who do something grand or very noble for the town, and, it is a very rare award to receive," The Mayor informed.

"So, as you would expect, we can't give you the award again..." he chuckled.

"So, especially for you we have created a new award."

A wave of 'oohs' and 'aahs' went around the garden; everyone was listening intently to hear what the new award was.

"It is called the Oak Town's Gold Award of Gratitude!" announced the Mayor, joyously.

There was an applause before the Mayor went over to a small wooden table that was in the corner of the pop-up stage and picked up two beautifully crafted Oak boxes; on the lids of both boxes there were a hand engraved Oak Trees and underneath there was a rectangle – with especially swirly corners – and inside the rectangle it said: Oak Town Award.

Heather and Nate's eyes widened in happiness and excitement. The Mayor nodded encouragingly at them and gestured for them to open the beautifully handcrafted boxes.

Heather and Nate opened the boxes and gasped when they saw what was inside...

Inside the boxes there were two absolutely magnificent medals. The medals were gold and large, they had one acorn on them and beautiful oak leaves decorated around the outside... On the top of the medals each of them had Heather and Nate's name on top.

Heather and Nate heartily thanked the Mayor but the Mayor just warmly said: "Thank you, Heather and Nate."

After that, there was a roaring applause and Heather and Nate bowed before the Mayor said: "Now everyone! Let's have our picnic!"

Heather and Nate went up first: they both picked up a large paper plate and walked down beside the table and helped themselves to the food. After that, they put their plates down on their picnic blanket and then they went back round with two more plates and chose some dessert and then both sat down... After that, a queue formed as everyone else went along to get their food. The queue stretched all around the garden – but it was worth it!

Soon, everyone was happily seated back down with their food and chatted merrily. Heather and Nate were seated at a picnic blanket that had miniature Oak trees on it and were sitting with: their parents, Grandparents, Aunt and Uncle, two cousins (called Jack and Lucy) and even the Mayor! ... Every five minutes, people would come and congratulate Heather and Nate for saving Oak Town once more...

The picnic party went on until around five o'clock and then the guests slowly began to leave. It was around six by the time everyone left; and, as they did some guests gave gifts to Heather and Nate – as a thank you for the picnic or as a thank you for saving the town! They both thanked the townsfolk for coming and finally their Grandparents, Aunt and Uncle and Cousins left. After that, the police officers left and thanked them heartily. Then, it was just the Mayor. Once again, the Mayor thanked Heather and Nate before he too left...

"Well, you two have both saved the town again!" exclaimed Mum, proudly!

"We will be sure to treat you two with a trip of some sort!" Dad told them.

"After all, you still have two weeks left of the holidays!" he added.

Heather and Nate's eyes widened with excitement and happiness.

"Thank you!"

"Thanks!" they both beamed.

And, so Heather and Nate both did enjoy the rest of their day – however, the criminals did not enjoy their day on the other hand! They were all in prison and Jenny – for some reason – was very pleased! But Dan and Claude were not pleased in the slightest!

EPILOGUE

That evening, Heather and Nate were in their tree house and talked about their adventure... Heather and Nate both imagined having loads of other adventures in the future. And they will! But, those would be other stories...

BOOKS IN THIS SERIES

The Great Escapes

Nate and Heather are brother and sister, they live an ordinary life in an ordinary town - until now... When they are on a trail of criminals they realize the fate of their town is in their hands... From a ship wreak at the bottom of a lake, a tumble down castle, an abandoned house and an island with many secrets - will they be able to escape them all to save their town - before it's too late...

The Great Escape

Nate and Heather are brother and sister. They live an ordinary life until now. When they find a secret letter in the woods it takes them on an adventure, one that they certainly weren't expecting and they soon realise that the fate of their town is in their hands... Will two ordinary children be able to save the town? Before it is too late...

The Escape Across The Ocean

Heather and Nate are looking forward to a holiday in Northern Oak Town. Although, like last year, they get swept in another adventure... Three criminals are spreading counterfeit money across Oak Town. But how? However, when trying to solve the case, Heather and Nate get captured - and imprisoned... From being imprisoned in an abandoned house with: a secret room and a secret passageway. And, being prisoner on an island of many secrets... Heather and Nate must find a way to escape, from the three criminals, and save the town, before it is too late...

ABOUT THE AUTHOR

Riya Musthyala

 My name is Riya Musthyala, I am 13 years old and I live in England. My favourite authors are: Chris Colfer and M.G Leonrad & Sam Sedgeman. I enjoy writing adventure and fantasy stories and novels... I hope you enjoy reading my book!

Printed by Amazon Italia Logistica S.r.l.
Torrazza Piemonte (TO), Italy

40702037R00107